# THE FACE OF FURY

An apparently law-abiding citizen is murdered in his London home, and a seemingly innocent young girl knifed to death in a London park. Both victims have their roots in Ulster and revenge and vendetta follow too fast for police detection to grasp what is really happening. When a mysterious booby-trap explosion causes horrendous loss of innocent lives, detectives still have difficulty in identifying the motive and apprehending the suspect. They are aware that a vengeful S.A.S. man has arrived in town from Ulster and find themselves having to grapple with the devious complexity of Irish politics...

# THE FACE OF FURY

# THE FACE OF FURY

*by*

## P. A. Foxall

**Dales Large Print Books**
Long Preston, North Yorkshire,
BD23 4ND, England.

British Library Cataloguing in Publication Data.

Foxall, P.A.
    The face of fury.

    A catalogue record of this book is
    available from the British Library

    ISBN   1-84262-109-2 pbk

First published in Great Britain 1982 by Robert Hale Limited

Copyright © P.A. Foxall 1982

The moral right of the author has been asserted

Published in Large Print 2002 by arrangement with
Robert Hale Ltd.

Dales Large Print is an imprint of Library Magna Books Ltd.

Printed and bound in Great Britain by
T.J. (International) Ltd., Cornwall, PL28 8RW

# ONE

Detective Sergeant Shindler of Catford
C.I.D. was accustomed to philosophising
when a villain met a nasty death in the
course of some brutal and squalid trade war
with his peers: 'It couldn't have happened to
a better man,' or 'At least we'll never have to
arse about the law courts again for him,
getting slanged by his brief and our balls
chewed off by the Judge, and then watch the
bastard walk away smirking after another
classic legal triumph and another famous
miscarriage of Justice.'

But when Ian Melling, a prosperous
Catford bookmaker was found one night,
dead in his bath, in his luxury flat overlooking Lewisham Park, Shindler could
only shake his head in sad and weary
resignation, suspending his usual spoken
epitaph until it was definitely established
that Melling had been a villain.

Certainly the manner of his passing was
appropriate to one who moved and dealt in
very dubious company. Both bath taps had

been turned full on, the water cascading down on Melling, until the bath overflowed and the water seeped through the floor into the flat below, dripping on the occupants in their bed until they raised the alarm. There was never any doubt about Melling's decease being an act of cold-blooded murder, even though the prime cause of death was drowning, and Melling was known to be a heavy drinker who might well have upended himself in the bath in the throes of an alcoholic stupor.

Prior to drowning, Melling had been knocked about by some specialist who knew how to inflict the maximum pain. There was a pattern of horrifying bruises covering most of his torso, resulting in liver, spleen and kidney damage as well as several broken ribs. Moreover the telephone wire leading out of his apartment had been cut, and the heavy outer door, protected by a dead bolt, had been jemmied open. Melling must have died many deaths in the small hours as he cowered in his room like a rat in a hole, with his telephone dead and no way out, listening to the splintering of wood on the outer door as a ruthless enemy broke in to attack him.

It was obvious that revenge and not robbery was the motive, for nothing else in the flat had been touched.

The rooms were expensively over-furnished in a rather tasteless manner. There were glass-fronted display cabinets filled with silver cups and sporting trophies, and the walls were hung with the framed coloured prints of famous horses and jockeys, former Derby and Grand National winners, as became a great lover of the Sport of Kings.

None of the personal or business papers in Melling's desk appeared to have been touched, and none of his drawers or cupboards had been ransacked. Apart from the body in the bath and the splintered outer door, the normal lived-in tidiness of the comfortable flat offered no other evidence that it had been ravished by a violent intruder who had left no finger-prints. But the infra-red scanner showed some alien foot impressions in the deep-piled carpeting of size ten shoes. Melling took a size seven, so the large prints with the ridged pattern of commonplace plastic-soled sneakers on sale everywhere in their thousands must have belonged to the murderer.

'What do you make of it so far?' said Detective Chief Inspector Sperling, when Shindler came into his office with his initial report from the scene of the crime. 'Does it look like death inflicted in the course of robbery?'

'That's not how it stacks up to me, guv. Nothing's been touched apart from Melling himself. He still had a hundred quid in his wallet, and there's plenty of good portable silverware in the flat that's been left. The killer was a violent psychopath. He had it in for Melling, and really made him suffer before he drowned him. Here's the preliminary medical report with a list of probable injuries; like an accident report from a motorway pile-up.'

'A settling of old scores then,' sighed the chief inspector. 'Some villain he must have crossed. Any idea if Melling belonged to that side of the tracks?'

'Couldn't say for sure yet, guv. There have been one or two odd whispers about him from snouts.'

'What sort of whispers?'

'That he was into the race-track rackets, horse-doping and you name it. But nothing was ever found heavy enough to stick to him. As far as we know he made his money legitimately in the Curzon Road betting shop. I've got a man down there now interviewing his employees.'

'Did he live alone in his flat?'

'The neighbours all seem to think so. None of them remembers seeing a woman go in there for some time. But in the built-in wardrobe of the main bedroom there's a whole rack full of female dresses and coats and shoes, with all the attendant smells. It looks as if he had a woman there once, or set it up for her to come, but if she ever moved in she moved out again some time ago.'

'How long has he lived in that particular apartment block?'

'About three years, according to the land-lord's agents. He moved up market from a more modest pad in Mount Pleasant Road. I suppose his betting shop or his other money-spinners had started to prosper.'

'And how long has he been in our manor altogether?'

'About eight years. And you're not going to like this, guv. Melling is from Northern Ireland – Belfast. He suddenly appeared in Catford in seventy-three with enough ready money to set up as a licensed bookmaker, and he's never looked back, till last night.'

The chief inspector gave him an inscrutable look.

'You're damned right I don't like it,' he declared flatly. 'A vicious, revenge-type killing of a bloody Irishman, with all that that implies! As if we haven't got enough trouble already with the pissed-off blacks and their commie organisers! The Irish dimension I can certainly do without. That insane asylum spilling over on our streets would be the absolute end. You'd better find out pretty damned quick who this Melling really was, and if he was into anything heavy in the political or sectarian line. Have you checked with the R.U.C. yet?'

'No, guv.'

'Well, see to it. Send them a full description with his finger-prints. And while you're at it, consult with the Anti-Terrorist Squad and Special Branch, on the off-chance that Melling has ever crossed their path. Keep me fully informed.'

When Shindler had made the prescribed enquiries, his report to his superior was far from reassuring.

'You said you didn't want that Irish mess spilling over on our streets, guv. Well, it looks as if you've got it. The Ulster police have known all about this joker since sixty-nine. His real name was Kiernan O'Malley, and he was a hard-line republican, thought to be a quartermaster for the Provisional I.R.A., but they could never get enough evidence to put him away. Nobody ever had the bottle to testify against him, and the Army always had urgent business in the other direction when he swaggered about at Sinn Fein rallies in Belfast with his black beret and dark glasses, brandishing an M60 machine gun.'

'What exactly do you mean by I.R.A. quartermaster?' said Sperling.

'He raised funds for their war chest by robbing banks. He ran a full-scale protection racket throughout the business community of West Belfast. Shopkeepers, pub landlords, club owners, even market traders paid off a levy to the bagman. If they didn't they got knee-capped by O'Malley's thugs. Everybody knew it was going on, but the police were powerless to stop it. None of the pigeons dared make a complaint, and if the undercover police managed to catch a bagman in the act, they got nothing out of him. His place was taken next day by another bandit.'

'What happened in nineteen seventy-three to bring O'Malley over here as a bookmaker?'

'He was into sectarian killings in retaliation for the murder of some Irish Catholics by the Prots. A minibus carrying a dozen protestant workers from a factory outside Belfast was ambushed on a country road by an I.R.A. squad reputed to have been led by O'Malley. The prots were lined up against the van with their hands on their heads and cut down by sub-machine guns. It was a re-run of the St. Valentine's Day massacre in Chicago by Al Capone, a terrible atrocity even by Irish standards. The victims left behind a dozen widows and about thirty orphans. So the prots were hopping mad, and their assassination squads were out to get O'Malley at all costs.

'They shot his brother-in-law and two of his neighbours by mistake, trying to get him. Then they wired up a bomb in his car, but his wife happened to borrow it that morning to go to the market, so she was killed instead. O'Malley knew then that Belfast was too hot to hold him, so he took off to London under the name of Ian Melling.'

'H'm,' commented the chief inspector. 'It ought not to be possible for retired terrorists from Ulster to hang up their boots and turn respectable in London without somebody knowing.'

'Special Branch and the Bomb Squad, as it was then, were tipped off by the R.U.C.,

14

and they kept a close watch on Ian Melling. But after a year or two, when they saw he made no attempt to contact any of the known republican activists over here, and showed no sign of raising any mayhem, they left him alone. He set up his betting shop with funds from an unspecified source – probably what he siphoned off from the I.R.A. bank robberies he organised, and concentrated on making money legitimately. He's been a burnt-out case for years politically, and now all of a sudden he gets his come-uppance on our manor.'

'I'm keeping an open mind on whether it was a revenge killing with its roots in Ulster,' said the chief inspector. 'If it was, it seems to have taken the protestant assassin an awful long time to track him down.'

'Par for the course with that lot, guv. There's probably an Irish joke about it.'

'Does the R.U.C. have any ideas about protestant hard men who've recently come to London?'

'No, guv. They wouldn't give me any names even if they knew. They're not exactly going into mourning over O'Malley. He was their Public Enemy Number One for years.'

'Even so, I want this case cleared up,' said Sperling. 'I'm not having some sneaky bastard from Belfast coming here to settle an old score and walking off with impunity. Before we know where we are we'll have a long-running Irish vendetta unfolding before our eyes, leaving bodies all over the streets and tying up all our available manpower. Contact the Anti-Terrorist Squad at the Yard, and ask if they've any knowledge of a suspicious character or two coming in from Belfast lately.'

'O.K., guv.'

'And go round all your snouts for anything out of the ordinary. Check the rooming houses, doss-houses and cheap hostels. If there's any report of a strange mick in the area during the past week, follow it up and bring him in for questioning.'

'Anything else, guv?'

'You say you've got all you can from Melling's employees. What about his other contacts and associates, especially that woman who's left a wardrobe full of clothes in the flat? Also I want to know more about his funds from an unspecified source, because that's another term for criminal conniving.'

'I daresay there are plenty of well-off republican sympathisers in London who'd be only too glad to put up the money to stake a famous old Belfast thug like

16

O'Malley,' observed Shindler

'So talk to his bank manager. If he's officious about the secrets of the confessional, we can get a court order to examine the account particulars now that O'Malley is a murder victim. Let's not rule out the possibility that O'Malley could have been up to his neck over here in the usual quest for a fast buck, and the old Irish connection could be a red herring, guaranteed to send us off in the wrong direction.'

## TWO

Detective Constable Frank Neilson, who'd been sent down to Melling's Turf, the betting shop in Curzon Road near the Greyhound Stadium, found the establishment open for business as usual and doing its regular brisk trade with the unemployed, even though its founder-owner was no more.

The manager in charge was Frank Robbie, a small, rotund, round-faced Southern Irishman, with a drinker's belly and a hearty raucous laugh. He was fat, sly and jovial, and his infectious good humour made even the dedicated losers feel slightly less disgruntled.

'Ah,' he said, with a distinct cooling of bonhomie at the sight of Neilson's warrant card. 'Himself is not in the office yet, sorr. Running a wee bit late this morning, so he is. Ten o'clock he's generally here for when we put the boards up. Is it anything that I can be seeing to, officer?'

'You mean you've not heard yet?' said Neilson.

'Heard what?'

'About your guv'nor, Mr Melling.'

'And what would that be that I've not heard, sorr?'

'He's dead.'

'Holy-Jesus-and-Mary!' gasped Robbie, turning pale. 'What's that you said?'

'It happened during the night. Somebody broke into his flat near Lewisham Park and drowned him in his bath.'

'No!'

'The water overflowed and dripped through the floor on the people underneath. They raised the alarm at three-thirty, and we were there shortly after.'

'I can't believe it,' moaned Robbie with his head in his hands. 'Such a fine gentleman as Mr. Melling. Terrible, terrible people in this

18

city, so there are.'

'Do you know if anybody had ever threatened him? Any of the punters who thought they'd been short-changed?'

'Surely not!' retorted the manager indignantly. 'I see to it we run a clean shop. There's never been a dissatisfied customer here, and that's the truth of it.'

'How long have you known Mr. Melling?'

'Three years it is I've worked for him here, and never a cross word.'

'What about before then?'

'Sure I never knew the man before I came to work for him.'

'Did you ever hear anything about his other business activities?'

'What others? I don't know what you mean?' said the manager, suddenly becoming quiet and withdrawn. 'What would you be getting at, officer?'

'I mean connections with sharp buggers who bend the law,' said Neilson impatiently. 'Isn't it that sort of business, dealing with the scum, that gets men drowned in their bath?'

'I wouldn't be knowin' about that, sorr. But sure you're misjudging the poor man something terrible if you're thinking that of him.'

'I presume he was married.'

'A widower, so he was.'

'Since when?'

'I heard he lost his wife in the troubles before he came across the water.'

'Go on,' said Neilson with new interest. 'What else have you heard about him?'

'No more than that, sorr.'

'And why did he come here from over the water?'

'You'd have to ask himself that, poor gentleman,' retorted Robbie. 'Sure there's nobody else would be likely to know.'

'Oh, yes, there is,' said Neilson grimly. 'The sod who worked him over and dunked him in his bath.'

'May the good Lord forgive him for his black soul,' intoned the manager piously.

'Was Melling keen on women?' said Neilson suddenly.

'Now there's a very peculiar question,' said Robbie, giving him a shifty look. 'Sure he was a warm and passionate man, and why should he not?'

'There was a whole wardrobe full of women's clothes in Melling's flat. Who do you suppose they might belong to?'

'Sure they'd belong to his young sister, Kathleen,' said Robbie. 'I understand he

20

was very close to her. And sometimes she'd come over on a visit from Belfast for a rest from the troubles. She'd leave a set of clothing in Mr. Melling's flat so as not to be always carrying big suitcases with her.'

'How old would she be?'

'Still in her twenties, and quite a dish of a girl.'

'You've seen her then?'

'To be sure I saw her once in Mr. Melling's car. He stopped outside the shop on his way back from a race meeting at Fontwell Park to check everything was still running all right here. He saw me looking at her through the window there, and told me she was his little sister Kathleen, come over from Belfast to stay with him for a wee holiday from the troubles.'

'Is that all he said about her?'

'Sure, and if he said any more, I can't remember it now.'

'How long is it since you saw her here?'

'It must be a twelve-month since, maybe more.'

'And has Melling ever mentioned her coming to stay since then?'

'No, sorr. But he'll not be confiding in me his domestic arrangements, will he now?'

'Could you help our Identikit man to

21

build up a likeness of Kathleen Melling?' said Neilson.

'No, sorr. I'm sorry I could not.'

'You mean you won't help us?'

'Sure I'll help you as far as lies in me power. But I only saw the girl for half a second, so I did – enough to see she was young and pretty with long black hair – but I couldn't pick her out from a roomful of other young, pretty girls with long black hair, if you take my meaning, sorr.'

'All right,' sighed Neilson resignedly. 'How many other people have you got working here?'

'Three checkers, a typist and a cashier.'

'I'll see them in this office,' said the detective. 'Send them in one at a time.'

Sifting through the reports that had already come in on the Melling case, Detective Chief Inspector Sperling paused and re-read the one from Neilson on Kathleen Melling. Then he picked up the telephone and dialled the number of the R.U.C. Headquarters in Belfast. Having been put through to the Criminal Records Department, he asked a couple of questions about O'Malley, and waited patiently for the answers. When he replaced the receiver there was a gleam of renewed interest in his eye, and he sent immediately for Detective Sergeant Shindler.

'That woman who left her clothes in Melling's flat definitely wasn't his sister,' he stated flatly. 'Neilson was led up the garden path. Melling was forty-three years old. He came from a republican family of six. His two brothers are currently serving life sentences in The Maze for terrorist offences. His three sisters are all dustbin-rattling harridans in their thirties, tied down with hordes of kids, and they live in the Divis Flats on Social Security. There isn't a young, pretty, unmarried sister in her twenties, called Kathleen, with long black hair, a wardrobe of full expensive clothes, and the means to commute regularly between Belfast and London.'

'Far enough,' nodded Shindler. 'So she was his fancy piece, but he had his reasons for passing her off as his sister.'

'It's irrelevant anyway. What interests me is where she is right now, and why she left all that expensive gear in his flat. If they'd parted for good, surely she'd have taken it with her.'

'Maybe she really does commute between London and Belfast, and her mission is neither sexual nor fraternal,' suggested Shindler.

'We'll soon check on that. The finger-prints found on that wardrobe in Melling's flat must be hers. And if she was ever in-volved with him in Ulster, they've probably got her dabs on file. We'll get copies off to the R.U.C. by telex, and maybe we'll get a make on her.'

Two days later the reply came from Belfast, together with a police photograph of a young woman taken some nine years ago. She was undoubtedly good-looking, with a softly rounded face and pronounced Cupid's bow. But the total effect was spoilt by the glaring fanaticism of her close-set dark eyes. The finger-prints submitted from London had been matched up to show she was a republican woman terrorist called Kathleen Donoghue, now aged twenty-eight, wanted for questioning about the bombing of a Belfast restaurant in nineteen seventy-two, in which half a dozen people had been killed and as many others horribly maimed. She was believed to be hiding out in the Irish Republic.

There followed a résumé of her activities since nineteen sixty-nine when, as a school-girl of sixteen, she'd hurled petrol bombs at

24

the police and had torn up paving stones to be broken up for missiles. In between her frenzied bouts of political activity, she'd attended The Queen's University to train as a teacher. But she'd been arrested at her college and had done a year in prison for possessing a firearm.

She then attracted the attention of Kiernan O'Malley and became his pupil, protégée and mistress. She was thought to have been with him as courier, bed-warmer, bomb-carrier and general factotum on several of his suspected atrocities. Apart from the restaurant outrage, one crime in particular, the enticement and massacre of four off-duty soldiers, had put her high on the wanted list in Belfast. But she'd bolted to the Republic, from where she couldn't be extradited on political grounds, and it was thought she'd been living there ever since.

There was no information forthcoming from Dublin on her activities, but it now looked as if she'd been travelling between London and Dublin undetected for years, to meet Kiernan O'Malley in his Catford flat. What she'd come for, other than a sexual attachment, to see the veteran terrorist in retirement, was open to speculation.

However, the R.U.C. and Scotland Yard's

Anti-Terrorist Squad were still convinced that O'Malley was a burnt-out case who hadn't participated in any act of terror or political subversion during the eight years he'd lived in London.

'So what the hell's been going on?' said the chief inspector impatiently. 'Is that bitch over here now or in Dublin? And what light is she likely to be able to throw on O'Malley's murder?'

'It looks to me as if those two shits have been fooling the Special Branch and the Anti-Terrorist Squad for years,' growled Shindler. 'It doesn't shatter me with grief that he got drowned in his bath. I'm worried about what could still be going down under our noses. We're too complacent by half in this country. Bombers, hoodlums and murderers, they just come and go as they please. They even vote in our General Elections. And look at old Mountbatten, going over there to spend his holidays among them, for Christ's sake! He thought they couldn't be bothered to knock him off just because he was a geriatric! So what about this Kathleen Donoghue, guv? Are we going to make her a priority enquiry?'

'Yes, we'd better have her picture circulated,' replied Sperling morosely, 'for all the good it'll do. If we got the slightest co-operation from Dublin, we might have some idea what she's been up to. But I don't reckon she'll show her face over here again for some time now the heat's on.'

## THREE

Sergeant James Montgomery Faldo of the S.A.S. Regiment was slim, wiry and tautly muscular, with a brisk military bearing that denoted years of training. In fact, at the age of thirty he'd spent nearly as much time in the army as out of it, having joined a Junior Leader's Regiment in his teens and then gone into the regular army where he'd signed on for twelve years. His father had been sergeant major in a Guards Battalion during World War Two, so the young Faldo had been brainwashed with military lore and former glory from the time he could take anything in. He was standing to attention and saluting before he could walk and talk properly.

The Army had always been his life, and he could never envisage making a go of it in civvie street. But things had turned sour on him since the Irish business and the three tours of duty he'd done in Ulster with the Parachute Regiment and later with the S.A.S. He had scores to settle, and such accounts could never be paid in full while he was a serving soldier. Besides, Jim Faldo didn't think he'd been fairly treated in the Army. Trouble sought him out. He'd been busted twice from corporal down to private, and it had taken years of keeping his nose clean to work his way up again.

It was always the bloody Irish who caused his downfall. The first time, at the start of his tour in Ulster, when he hadn't realised the intensity of the tribal hatred there, he'd been having a quiet off-duty drink in a pub in West Belfast, when a couple of young tearaways from the Creggan had spotted him as a Brit in disguise, and set about picking a fight. The pub was wrecked. The two tearaways went off in an ambulance, and Corporal Faldo went off to the cooler, from which he emerged via a Court Martial, shorn of his rank and consigned to the doghouse.

After a year of conscientious service he won his promotion back again. But while on foot patrol in the Bogside, he'd chased and captured a Provisional who took a couple of shots at him from an alley and then had his pistol jam. Somewhere in between being handed over to the R.U.C. and being seen by his solicitor, the Provo had sustained two black eyes, a missing row of front teeth and a broken jaw. He swore that his injuries had been inflicted by the paratrooper who jumped on him in the Bogside. So Corporal Faldo found himself on another Court Martial which piously reduced him to the ranks again.

Being now a marked man for brawling and brutality in the Paras, Faldo knew his only hope of promotion was a transfer to another unit. He applied for the S.A.S., and somewhat to his surprise they accepted him, in spite of, or perhaps because of, his established image.

It could be said that the brutal war in Ireland had dehumanised him. He was brave, ultra-cynical about humanity, and completely ruthless. Perhaps it was the only way he could function in his chosen trade, and he did so well with the S.A.S. that he was a sergeant within three years.

Shortly afterwards his twelve years with the Colours expired, but Sergeant Faldo ignored the blandishments and the offers of promotion if he'd sign on for another twelve years. He grabbed his gratuity and all the back pay coming to him, and ran. He was determined to do things his own way in future. In Ulster he'd seen the world from the bottom side up, and anywhere else must be an improvement.

He arrived in Euston Station from Liverpool, dressed in Khaki trousers and green camouflage jacket, with his meagre belongings packed in a regulation large valise. He also carried a sack-like canvas kitbag with his name and number stencilled on it, which he handled very carefully as if it was full of delicate and valuable merchandise.

He was not a particularly good-looking man with his short-cropped sandy hair, his cold, green, cat-like eyes, his hawk-like nose and tight, thin-lipped mouth, all of which combined to give him the lean and hungry look of a street fighter. He had a certain savage charisma which made other men immediately look to him in moments of supreme danger.

Faldo hailed a taxi outside the station and gave the driver an address in Camberwell, the home of his younger brother who was his only surviving relative.

Harry Faldo, two years younger than Jim,

and subjected to the same parental con-
ditioning, had also made the Army his
career. But he was softer, clever with his
hands and less aggressive than his brother.
Because of his technical aptitude he was
drafted into the Royal Corps of Signals to
repair and maintain radio equipment.

Within a couple of months of arriving in
Belfast Harry Faldo was shot down in an
I.R.A. ambush and left for dead. Hit by four
machine gun bullets, he had only the
faintest flicker of life left in him, which the
medics managed to prevent from going out.
After a year of intensive care and numerous
operations, and therapy spread over several
more years, he recovered a limited use of his
paralysed legs, and was just able to stagger
along painfully slowly with the aid of a
couple of sticks. He was then discharged
from the Army with the usual pittance,
laughingly called a Disability Pension. He
returned to Ireland to marry the Catholic
girl who'd helped nurse him back to life in
the Royal Victoria Hospital in Belfast.

She came from a respectable area in the
Antrim Road, where Protestants and
Catholics lived side by side like people. Her
father was landlord of a staunchly Catholic
pub, The Green Dragon, which had never

been bombed.

Having had what was virtually a secret wedding, the young couple had to get far away from Ulster before the tribal bigots permanently dissolved the new marriage. So they came to Camberwell and, with their limited resources, took a small shop in a rundown district near the Wandsworth Road, where Harry Faldo set up in business as a clock-maker. It was a skill he'd developed as a hobby during his boyhood, of finding broken old clocks and making them work again. He was now just an ordinary humble man, trying to get from day to day.

The taxi threaded its way through the mean streets of a typical twilight city zone, to a place near the railway line, with boarded up shops, empty offices, derelict factories and raw open demolition sites. In a dark street opposite a sleazy tenement block with scummy tiles on the outside, was a gaunt narrow shop with a single bay window containing a shelf full of assorted old clocks for sale. There was the inscription: HARRY FALDO CLOCKMAKER on a sign above the door.

The walls had the rough stuccoed look of flaking plaster, and the paintwork was chipped like archaeological excavations. The people on the streets, West Indians and poor whites in roughly equal proportions, had that unmistakable aura of feckless and shiftless human flotsam, with unemployment and the weekly dole as a way of life.

Jim Faldo looked about him with a grimace of distaste, and decided that you could come down in the world even from Belfast, which he'd always thought of as the arsehole of the world. But then, poor old Harry was never going to set the world on fire. With his gimpy legs and his Irish bitch wife, there wasn't much else he could do but flog botched-up old clocks to no-hopers in condemned houses.

As the rickety shop door opened with the clang of a cracked bell, Harry Faldo looked round from his work bench, where he was dismantling the old, corroded movement of a grandfather clock.

He had the same sandy hair and greenish eyes as his older brother, but his face was more softly rounded and had a slightly sick pallor. The jaw was not aggressive and the mouth was more suited to smiling. His eyes had a gentle conciliatory expression with no light in them, as if a part of him had died with the shooting.

'Hullo, Jim,' he exclaimed, tottering to his feet and extending his hand. 'You found us then. What was the journey like?'

'Bloody awful,' said his brother. 'Are you making out then?'

As he spoke he glanced all round him with a keen ironic look that said he could see for himself.

'We're making a living, just about,' said Harry. 'Things are a bit tight. Not many people round here can afford a long-case clock. But trade has picked up since we opened.'

'How's Bernadette?'

'We've got a third boy now. Rory, three months old. I think I told you in my letter.'

'Three in less than three years, eh,' said Jim. 'That's about right for a good Catholic girl. Are you going for a football team then?'

Harry laughed politely. His morose and abrasive older brother had always made him feel nervous and ill-at-ease. You never knew what tasteless and hurtful remark he was going to come out with next.

'Have you got anything particular in mind now you're a civvie?' said Harry. 'I mean anything in the way of a job.'

'You mean how long am I likely to inflict myself on you. Well, you can reassure

Bernadette it's not going to be a long stay.'

'That's not what I meant. She's got your room ready, and you can stay as long as you like. Bernadette has no objection at all. She knows you're all the family I've got.'

'Well, don't fool yourself about who we are and the label they've stuck on us. No bloody clever politician or do-gooder is ever going to wipe that away.'

'You mean because she's Catholic Republican, and you're S.A.S.?'

'In a nutshell.'

'But Bernadette's not like that. We agreed when we married to put all the hate behind us. Politics and old grievances are taboo in this house. It's the only way to have a normal, decent life. What did it ever get anybody, all the pointless killing and savagery?'

'A very good question. You should put it to those bloody subhuman micks who pulled the ambush at Warren Point last year.'

'How did you like the S.A.S.?'

'You know I'm not allowed to discuss it. Even after we've signed off we're under oath to remain anonymous.'

'But you fitted in all right, I'll bet. Just up your street, wasn't it? I don't really see you settling down to a dull, humdrum life in civvie street after the kind of action you've been enjoying for years.'

'Is that a fact?' said Jim. 'Maybe you're right.'

'So why have you left the army? And why do you want to stay in London for a couple of weeks? Don't try to con me it's warm family feeling or fraternal solidarity. We've never been all that close, and you never approved of me marrying a Catholic girl from Belfast. You made no secret of it either. So why are you here, Jim? What are you up to?'

'Maybe I can do my job for a time better as a freelance than having to account for my every move to some toffee-nosed prick of an officer, who still thinks the war is a jolly sporting house match at his public school.'

'And what's your job going to be?' said Harry tensely. 'Your usual? Killing micks?'

'The less you know about it the better. You've just said you're ready to forgive and forget, even though they shot you down like a bloody rat and left you a gimp for the rest of your life.'

'Come on, Jim,' persisted his brother. 'Level with me. If you're going to stay under my roof I've got a right to know what you're up to. I won't betray you. You know that.'

'And what about Bernadette? She's still part of the Irish mafia. She'd soon finger me to some local Sinn Fein stoolie.'

'She won't hear a word about it from me, I swear. A man has to keep certain things secret from his wife or civilised living wouldn't be possible.'

'Well, you're the expert on that,' conceded his brother.

'So what are you doing in London, Jim? Who are you after?'

'All right, if you must know. It's that bloody murdering swine O'Malley that you know all about; hero of forty army deaths, mostly shot in the back or blown up by remote control. He's turned respectable and is living here in London, less than five miles from here. There's not enough real evidence against him even to give him a parking ticket. But we know what he's done out there since nineteen sixty-nine. Why should a bastard like that enjoy an honourable retirement among the fleshpots, with all the money he needs, and die peacefully in his bed? I know there's no justice in this world, but my God! O'Malley–'

'You're crazy!' exclaimed his brother aghast. 'You'll never get away with it, not in London. The police here have a good record for solving murders. It's not like Belfast, where they just sweep up the remains, have a gangster's funeral and then forget about it in anticipation of the next shooting. They'll sus you out and put you away for half your life. Don't think your S.A.S. glamour will cut any ice at an ordinary felony murder trial.'

'Give over, for Christ's sake!' scoffed Jim. 'How would they ever know it was me, unless I left a signed confession? There must be hundreds of men who've done their time in Ulster and have just as good a reason as I've got for taking out O'Malley. So why should they zero in on me? And don't tell me the London fuzz haven't got a whole batch of unsolved killings on their books.'

'But how do you know for sure O'Malley is in London? How do you know it's the right O'Malley? You never met him face to face, did you?'

'Oh, I know it's him all right. On patrol in Armagh a year ago we jumped his brother Padraig with three other punks, wiring up a bloody great bomb in a culvert for the next armoured personnel carrier that came through. When I realised we'd actually got one of the O'Malleys, I kicked the shit out of Padraig till he told me where his big brother's gone to ground. Kiernan's been hiding out in London since 'seventy-three under an alias, and he's got a bloody good

38

thing going for him. A betting shop in Catford making thousands. Melling's Turf, it's called. The word is that he's still in touch with that poisonous bitch Kathleen Donoghue, who screwed for him and suckered men to their deaths. She's gone to ground in London as well, and no doubt they get together over many a bottle of spud whisky and wallow like ghouls in their bloody memories. I'm going to take her out as well, if only for what she did to you.'

'No, Jim,' pleaded his brother. 'Not on my account. I don't bear any grudges. I'm just glad to be alive with my wife and three healthy boys, and forget all that.'

'Oh, for Christ's sake, where's your self-respect?' exclaimed the older Faldo irritably. 'She's the bitch who picked up you and your four mates in that Shankhill Road pub, pretending to belong to the Orange Order and very pro-Brit, and invited you all to a party where there were plenty of spare girls and booze. Remember? You were so wet behind the ears, you fell for it. So she took you to this nice house where there seemed to be a party going on. But the rightful owners were bound and gagged upstairs. It was an I.R.A. party. And when you trooped into this luxurious sitting room with the soft lights and sweet music, your tongues hang-ing out for free booze, and your flies unzipped for crumpet, there was O'Malley and his squad of goons waiting for you with sub-machine guns. They cut you down and you were the sole survivor. How many bullets did they dig out of you?'

'For God's sake, Jim, let it rest,' muttered Harry, with tiny beads of sweat breaking out on his upper lip at the naked horror of the memory. 'If I'm prepared to forget it, why can't you?'

'What! After she lured you to the slaughter, and left you a bloody hopeless cripple for the rest of your life! God knows how many others she served the same way, and it's on their account as well as yours that I'm going to cut her bloody throat. A pal of mine in the Dublin C.I.D. who used to be in the Irish Guards tipped me off that she's in London now, probably under an alias. You can bet your life she's in close touch with O'Malley, because she was always his bitch. He'll tell me her new name and where to find her before he buys the farm.'

'Jim,' pleaded his brother, 'please don't do it. Why make yourself as low and vile as they are? Even if they escape the physical penalty for what they've done, their real punishment that they can never escape is in being such shits and having to live with it.'

'That's too subtle for me. It sounds pretty wet as well.'

'Don't waste yourself on them. Leave them to the law.'

'Oh yes, the law! The law, dear brother, exists merely to protect the guilty from the consequences of their crimes, not to protect the innocent or avenge the victims. That has to be done by well-meaning amateurs like me. But if you feel too righteous to take a mere nuts-and-bolts man under your roof, I'll push on and find digs somewhere else.'

'No, stay here for a bit anyway,' said his brother. 'I owe you that at least. But I don't want to know about your plans for waging your own private war against expatriate micks.'

## FOUR

The living accommodation was on two storeys above the shop, which Harry Faldo held on a short lease from a West Indian landlord. At the front of the first floor facing

41

on to the street was a large living room with a kitchen alcove. It was cluttered with second-hand furniture and all the untidy paraphernalia of a household with a very young family.

There was a pram, a playpen and a high chair, and all sorts of plastic toys underfoot. There was a sleeping baby in the pram, a slightly older baby grizzling and whining in the playpen, and a toddler crawling about under the table, hammering on a saucepan with a wooden spoon. Their names were Ross, Roderick and Rory, and at Bernadette's insistence they'd all been baptised into the Catholic Church. Two of them had the sandy hair and greenish eyes of the Faldos, but the newest arrival had the dark hair and deep violet eyes of the Irish strain in Bernadette.

She was standing at the ironing board, flushed from her exertions, with a huge pile of ironed clothes stacked up before her and an equal amount still waiting in a laundry basket. She was short and sturdy with large hips and breasts, and her straight black hair was cut short. She had a round, cheerful, open face and good teeth, and her deep blue eyes had a soft tranquil quality. She smelt of scented soap, baby powder and baby vomit.

She was a nice, old-fashioned Catholic girl who'd tried hard to rid herself of the prejudices of her tribe when she married a British soldier and moved out of provincial life to the great metropolis.

Her carefully cultivated tolerance didn't extend to her husband's older brother Jim, whom she'd met only once before at the wedding, and decided he was a bad lot, one of the worst of the Brits, a real enemy of her people.

She greeted him civilly enough, but there was no warmth in her eyes. Jim Faldo nodded to her with a slightly ironical smile, thinking to himself that domestication had improved her. She was a splendid brood mare, born and bred for all the right functions. For a fleeting moment he actually envied his younger brother whom he'd always regarded with impatient condescension.

Bernadette spoke with the sing-song intonation of the Northern Irish in a soft, slightly husky voice.

'Welcome to our home,' she said briefly. 'I hope you'll be comfortable here. Your room's upstairs on the next floor. Will I be showing it to you now, while Harry puts the kettle on for a cup of tea?'

She unplugged her electric iron and led

43

the way up a narrow flight of stairs to the floor above, where there were three bedrooms. The room she showed him into was small and square with drab wallpaper, a threadbare carpet and a large old-fashioned double bed with clean linen and bedspread.

'You can use the wardrobe and chest of drawers for your gear,' she said. 'Two blankets should be enough this time of year. The bathroom's downstairs next to the kitchen. Anything else you want?'

'I can't think of anything right now. Thanks, Bernadette. You're a good sort.'

'Yes, I'd have to be, wouldn't I?' she retorted tartly. 'I don't want to be rude, Mr. Faldo, sorr. But how long would you be thinking of honouring us with your presence?'

'A week or two was what Harry suggested. If you want me out before, just say so. Shall I even bother to unpack?'

'Harry invited you, so that's all right by me. You're entitled to his hospitality. But let's not have any of your war games here, and let's not forget what you and your like have been doing to our people over the water. Christian forgiveness would have to be stretched a good long way to take no note of that. You're Harry's brother, but you've never really approved of him, have you?'

'What makes you say that?' said Jim Faldo, leaning his kitbag carefully against the wardrobe.

'I can tell. It's because he's not hard like you are. He's not a killer. He wasn't even a good soldier by your standards because he let himself be shot. Truth to tell, he should never have been in the Army. He's a decent, honest, peaceable man, so he is, an old softie, and that's all I ever want him to be. I don't want the likes of you bringing any trouble down on him.'

'Trouble!' exclaimed Jim. 'I'm out of the Army now, disarmed, harmless, clean. I couldn't get back into the Irish troubles even if I wanted to.'

'So you say!' she retorted sceptically. 'But I know your sort, you bloody macho heroes. You live on trouble and it follows you around. S.A.S. you call yourselves, but it's S.S. you're known as in the six counties. I pray to the good Lord that the leopard's changed his spots. That's all.'

'Thanks, Bernadette. You're a good soul,' said Jim with his wolfish smile. 'I'll not get Harry into any trouble, and I'll pay my way as a good lodger. I'm no free loader. I bet you can find a good use for the forty quid a week I'll be giving you while I'm here.'

'Och, bribery now is it then?' exclaimed Bernadette, considerably mollified. 'All right then, Mr. Faldo, sorr. We'll sign the peace treaty. And there's surely no need to tell Harry what I've just been saying, is there now?'

'Certainly not,' said Jim. 'We understand each other.'

'Tea up in five minutes then.'

When she'd gone, he looked round the drab bedroom that smelt of dry rot and damp wallpaper. He noted the large wooden crucifix hanging over the bed, and the framed embroidery text hanging on the opposite wall with the message: *Oh, Lord protect our home.*

'Poor little brother,' muttered Jim Faldo. 'The bloody Catholics have really taken him over.'

From the beginning of his stay in their home, Bernadette thought it strange that her brother-in-law didn't behave like a typical paid-off and discharged soldier with money burning holes in his pockets, and a whole city of the flesh-pots waiting just beyond the doorstep to be enjoyed. Jim Faldo stayed almost furtively in the house, generally up in

46

his bedroom reading paperback novels.

When he got bored with that, he came down into the living room to put the kettle on for a brew of tea. He never showed his face downstairs in the shop to fraternise with his brother's customers, and he never went into one of the numerous pubs in the neighbourhood. It was almost as if he was on the run and didn't want to be noticed. When he did go out it was never in the finery of the hunting male. He dressed in scruffy, casual clothes – faded blue jeans, logger's shirt and donkey jacket – so that he blended chameleon-like among the denizens of the twilight zone.

What his in-laws never knew was that he went out mainly at night when they were asleep. Although he'd been given a Yale key to the shop's front door, he didn't want his comings and goings monitored by his relatives, so he'd found his own exclusive exit down through one of the second floor windows at the back of the building. With his training it was easy enough to climb down a drainpipe fifteen feet on to the flat roof of an adjoining derelict shop, and thence through a broken skylight into the abandoned and vermin-infested interior of the decaying premises. After his night's excursion he returned to his bedroom by the same route, avoiding the tell-tale rattle of the shop's front door and the creaking boards on stairs and landing.

On the night when he paid his call in Catford he decided that the least conspicuous transport, with no risk of being traced afterwards, was his brother's rickety old N.H.S. invalid car that he kept in a lean-to shed in the small back yard behind the shop. With its crude, box-like body, its three small, inadequately sprung wheels and its five hundred c.c. motor bike engine, it was the crudest of basic transport. It chugged along erratically at twenty miles an hour, bouncing like a rubber ball and kept precariously on course by a tiller on the front wheel. It was the kind of vehicle that nobody would ever call to mind in association with a killer. Only poor cripples drove N.H.S. invalid cars.

Some time after midnight Jim Faldo wheeled the little buggy out of the yard like a pram and trundled it quietly down the street well out of earshot before he started up its noisy, petulant chattering motor. Then he chugged off to his rendezvous with the old I.R.A. killer five miles away.

When he returned an hour or two later, he

switched off the engine a quarter of a mile away and pushed the vehicle silently back into his brother's yard to its parking space under the lean-to shed. He re-entered the derelict premises next door, ascended to the roof and then climbed the last fifteen feet up the drainpipe to negotiate the top window of his brother's house.

He went to bed with a wild glow of triumph, conscious that he'd performed his grim task without being seen by a soul, either in transit to and fro, or at the place of execution. In the serenity of detachment, his night's work was a hell of a piece of action. He exulted in the way the murdering swine had wept and called on his God and pleaded for the mercy he'd never shown when he had a gun in his fist or a bomb under his jumper.

## FIVE

On the day after the murder of Ian Melling, Jim Faldo slept late and didn't surface till nearly midday. He came down for a pot of tea and some lunch, looking sleepy and self-satisfied with the contented surfeit of a well-filled predator.

'You're looking chipper and well pleased with yourself, as well as being bog-eyed,' commented Bernadette in her forthright manner. 'Out on the town all night, was it then?'

'Why? Did you hear me come in?'

'No, I never hear a damned thing, except when the baby cries. And the way you move around like a cat, I doubt if I'd hear you anyway.'

'I wasn't out last night,' said Jim shortly. 'It's the soft life and all the good meals I'm getting here that's making me look pleased. I'm still unwinding after my twelve years hard in the Army.'

'It's pleased I am to hear that,' said Bernadette tartly. 'Taking a fancy to a decent way of life, is it then?'

'It has its points.'

'Then you'll be thinking of getting yourself a job and turning respectable?'

'I might think about it,' he conceded.

'You'll be looking to get married then and setting up a real home?'

'Not very likely. That would be really pushing my luck,' he retorted flippantly. 'Marriage was invented by the Catholic

Church to make everybody as miserable as possible. I think I'll pass.'

'Och,' she replied bitterly. 'You'll never change, will you? You're a savage under the skin, so you are.'

Later that afternoon, when Harry Faldo looked at his copy of *The New Evening Standard*, his shocked eyes fastened on a prominent paragraph heading near the foot of the front page: CATFORD BOOK-MAKER MURDERED IN FLAT.

There followed a brief account of how Ian Melling, a betting shop proprietor, had been murdered in the night by an intruder in his Lewisham Park luxury flat. The police were anxious to hear from anybody who'd noticed any suspicious activity near the building during the small hours of the morning. In other words, they didn't know where to start looking for the assailant.

Recalling what Jim had told him about O'Malley owning a betting shop in Catford called Melling's Turf, Harry felt a sickening certainty that the murder victim was Kiernan O'Malley. His brother had actually carried out the murderous mission that had brought him to London.

Harry stuffed the newspaper inside his coat, and, leaning on his two walking sticks,

51

he tottered out along the landing and struggled desperately up the stairs to Jim's bedroom. His brother was relaxing, stretched out on the top of his bed reading a paperback thriller about a free-lance thug who successfully waged a murderous war single handed against the top celebrities of the *Cosa Nostra*.

He looked up, mildly curious, as Harry came staggering in, breathing hard, flushed from his exertions and tense with worry. He flicked the murder headline with the back of his hand.

'Is this it then?' he panted accusingly.

'Is this what?'

'This murder in Catford last night. Is it your intended hit on O'Malley that you told me about?'

'No comment.'

'Come on, Jim. You said O'Malley was a bookmaker. His name's Melling.'

'Well, you wouldn't expect a top Provo, known to the police and all the Protestant organisations in Ulster to live here openly under his own name.'

'Then it was you who killed him.'

'Leave it out. You're not involved.'

'I am involved. When you first came you told me what you were going to do.'

'You insisted on being told, didn't you? Seeing you here, a washed-up cripple by courtesy of O'Malley, and him living like a bloody Arab Sheik off his betting shop, set up by the I.R.A. murder funds, I thought you'd secretly be glad to have him knocked off.'

'Oh, Christ!'

'What's up?'

'If there's any fall-out from this Melling murder, it's going to come back here on all of us. I'm no freelance artist. I've got a wife and family to think of. I put five hundred miles between me and that insane slaughter-house in Ulster. And now you've brought it right back here on my doorstep.'

'Oh, give over!' exclaimed Jim impatiently. 'You've got no sense of proportion. We cheerfully accept the casual slaughter of six and a half thousand people on the roads every year, so why does everybody get so uptight when the micks kill a few dozen more in their primitive tribal wars? And why are you making such a song and dance over one bloodthirsty thug getting his lot? It's sheer hypocrisy. If you hadn't read that bloody newspaper, you wouldn't know anything about it.'

'Except what you told me the day you came.'

'Oh, forget that! Mere wishful fantasy. Did you hear me go out last night?'

'No.'

'Or come creeping back early this morning?'

'No.'

'Well then, as far as you're concerned I spent the night here in this bed. You know nothing. So stop worrying about some anonymous murder over in Catford that's nobody's business but that of the police. I'll be on my way soon and leave you in peace.'

'You mean after you've killed the woman, Kathleen Donoghue?' said Harry, tight-lipped.

'That slag!' said Jim indifferently. 'I haven't even found her yet. Forget about it. Get back to mending your clocks. That's a nice peaceful occupation for somebody who's had his mainspring broken by the micks.'

Harry stared at him for a moment, picked up his sticks and tottered out of the room.

On the landing outside he came face to face with Bernadette, who stood there petrified with horror, her eyes fixed on his with an incredulous nightmare expression of accusation and dread.

Neither husband nor wife had any sleep for most of that night, with the agonising recriminations and reproaches, the endlessly revolving, insoluble argument on what was to be done in the appalling dilemma in which they now found themselves.

'I knew it all along. Your bloody mad brother!' cried Bernadette malevolently. 'I just knew he was only here for some such dirty business. I always had him marked down as a vicious, bloodthirsty dog. I never wanted to give him house room. I told you he was trouble. But you kept on, and I let you talk me round! He's your only surviving relative, you said. Blood is thicker than water, you said. Aye, so it is. And so is that poor man's blood over in Catford, who'd be alive now if we hadn't harboured his bloody murderer.'

'Oh God!' groaned Harry. 'Please, Bernadette. Do stop going on about it for a bit. I'm trying to think.'

'Think is it! It's a bit late for thinking now, so it is. You know what we are now, the both of us? We're accessories to a foul murder. Yes, we are! By keeping that bloody scoundrel under our roof we're just as guilty as if we'd helped him to drown that poor man in his bath. We should go to the poliss, so we should. They're the only people to deal with bloody murder.'

'But we can't do that!' cried Harry desperately. 'We've got no proof that it was Jim. We're not even sure that he left the house last night. I never heard him. Did you?'

'No, but he could have gone all the same.'

'What kind of a shit would I be, setting the police on my own brother on the basis of a wild assumption? Besides, once you get those people on your back, snooping, harassing, prying, asking questions, suspicious of everybody, you're never free of them any more. If they did manage to pin that murder on Jim, they'd do us as well for harbouring him. They'd make us out to be as guilty as the murderer, bigger villains than the I.R.A.'

'And so we are!' cried Bernadette. 'That's what I've been saying. I feel as if my very own hands are stained with blood. What am I going to say to the Father when I'm in the confession box, and himself there listening to my sins, and me knowing I have this weight of mortal sin on my soul?'

'You can't go to confession and speak about that!' exclaimed Harry aghast.

'Can't I indeed! And who are you to tell

me to spit on the laws of God?'

'Couldn't you put off going to confession until Jim's left here? Then it won't matter what you tell the priest.'

'What!' squawked Bernadette furiously. 'And be denied the blessed sacrament for days and weeks while his lordship up there decides how long he's going to stay! You've got to tell him to go, Harry. That's all there is to it. We'll have no more truck with the likes of him.'

'But I can't do that,' objected Harry, who stood in too much awe of his brother to turn him out of the house. 'I can't go back on my word. And you're not to go stirring it up with him, Bernadette. You're supposed to know nothing at all about all this. You've jumped to too many conclusions already, most of them probably wrong. You can't try a man and convict him on suspicion alone, just because your woman's intuition tells you something about him that you don't like. There's every chance that Jim's innocent of this Catford murder.'

'So you say!' she scoffed. 'But then, you'd believe anything he wanted you to. I know what I think, and I know what ought to be done.'

So they went on for most of the night,

arguing acrimoniously in circles about the best thing to do. In the end, in complete emotional exhaustion, they fell asleep with nothing resolved.

## SIX

The uneasy *status quo* in the Faldo home continued. Bernadette regarded her brother-in-law with dread and revulsion, as if he were a time bomb ticking away to destruction.

She bided her time until he went out one afternoon, and then slipped into his bedroom looking for evidence of his capacity for murder. His sparse array of underwear and personal effects were laid out in the drawers of the chest with military tidiness. But it was the large bulky kitbag standing in the wardrobe that fascinated Bernadette. It wasn't padlocked, but the open end was pulled taut with a conventional drawstring, which she had no trouble in untying. She opened the kitbag and shone a torch inside. She didn't need any military experience to identify the contents and realise their significance.

Wrapped in a polythene bag were the stripped-down parts of a Sterling sub-machine gun, and three magazines loaded with 9 millimetre ammunition. Beneath that, veiled in a pair of black lace-trimmed knickers, was a Colt .45 automatic pistol as issued to the U.S. Navy. There was a .357 magnum revolver, a W.D. radio trans-mitter/receiver, a few 36 grenades, and several packages of plastic explosive to-gether with a separate box of detonators.

She didn't need to examine all the contents to know that Jim Faldo's kitbag was a veritable arsenal of deadly and destructive weapons, enough for a trained and determined man to fight his own vicious war. He must have stolen it from stores and armouries and captured I.R.A. arsenals during his service with the S.A.S.

Bernadette was pale and trembling as she pulled the drawstring tight again and re-arranged the kitbag in the same position as she'd found it. There was more fear than anger in her knowledge, and she didn't know what to do.

For a whole agonising day she kept her discovery to herself, shrinking from sharing it with her husband. She knew he was indecisive, lacking in true Catholic moral fibre, and scared of his brother. The awesome knowledge of that arsenal in the guest bedroom would merely be an additional source of anguished worry to him without prodding him to decisive action. Should she go to the police with her discovery, and how would it sour her future relations with her husband if she did? What she needed was a strong, decisive man to lean on, someone whose wisdom and fortitude would shore up her own fearful inadequacy, and give her the spiritual strength to do what was right. Who else could she turn to, being a good Catholic, but the local priest, Father Fogarty-Fegan, who'd baptised all her babies into the true church, and who heard her confession regularly once a week?

When the time came for the Father to be in his confessional at St. Patrick's Church, Bernadette put on her hat and coat, told Harry down in his shop to keep a listening ear for the sleeping children, and set out resolutely for her nearby spiritual home.

The church was a grandiose, baroque smoke-begrimed building dating from the nineteenth century, with tall steeple and belfry and a large expanse of stained glass windows in blue and red depicting the Holy Family with their golden haloes. It still dwarfed in its brash splendour the streets of tired, decayed little houses in its shadow, where the faithful congregation lived.

The church was empty on a weekday afternoon, apart from a few bowed figures in black, kneeling penitently in one of the pews near the altar. The solemn strains of church music rumbled through the lofty aisles as the organist practised his anthems and accompaniments. In the north transept were the six dark mahogany confession boxes, each containing a footstool for the kneeling penitent and a black curtain behind which the priest waited unseen to hear the whispered sins unfold.

Bernadette had to wait for a quarter of an hour until a grey, shabbily dressed, haunted man, looking sick with worry, came slinking furtively out of Father Fogarty-Fegan's confessional, and took himself off down the transept, forlorn and hopeless.

Bernadette crossed herself and knelt on the footstool in the claustrophobic space that smelt of decaying dust and incense, and the warm tobacco smell emanating from the priest. She made the sign of the cross again and announced herself to God's surrogate on earth.

'Bless me, Father, for I have sinned. I am

61

having unclean thoughts about my husband's brother, Jim Faldo, who has been staying in our house. Not by my wishes, but because my husband has invited him. I look at his powerful hands and the strength in his body, and the lustful thoughts come over me, Father, making me yearn for mortal sin with him. What am I to do?'

'My daughter,' intoned the priest solemnly, 'the sins of the mind are tolerable to God as long as they are bravely resisted. Even Our Blessed Lord was tempted by the Devil through his own thoughts. If the proximity of this man is not of your making, you can only continue to fight temptation with all the strength that God has given you. If your desire for purity is sincere, He will not let you fall. The flames of desire will eventually go away, and you will feel yourself doubly blessed for having fought the good fight.'

'But, Father,' she went on desperately, 'Jim Faldo is a terrible man, a man of violence, a member of the S.A.S. in Ulster. I overheard him talking to my husband about a bookmaker who's just been murdered in Catford. I know my husband suspects his brother of the crime. The bookmaker once lived in Belfast and was on the S.A.S. death list. I think we ought to tell everything to the poliss, but my husband is too loyal to his brother and does not agree. He says we have no proof, nothing but our suspicions which do not justify telling the poliss. If I report this man myself, what will it do to the relationship between me and my husband? Will he ever forgive me for betraying his brother who he's always looked up to? Father, what am I to do?'

'My daughter,' sighed the priest sadly, 'I am your spiritual adviser, and I can only advise you on matters relating to your immortal soul. Where the law and the police are involved, I have neither the knowledge nor the authority to advise you, especially where it concerns differences of opinion with your husband. Only you can know the closeness and the vulnerability of that relationship. You must pray for God's guidance, and act according to the dictates of your own conscience.'

'But, Father, Jim Faldo has guns, bombs and all sorts. I looked in his bedroom while he wasn't there. He's got a kitbag crammed full of pistols and bombs. What would he be doing with such things if not to kill more men on his S.A.S. death list? I heard mention of a woman he also threatened to kill. Should I tell the poliss about that, Father?'

There was a long silence behind the screen, and then the priest said:

'You must discuss it more thoroughly with your husband, and as the dangers are so clear and formidable, I'm sure that with God's help you will bring him round to your point of view. Certainly it would seem to be a citizen's prime duty to acquaint the police with the whereabouts of an arsenal of dangerous weapons in dubious hands. And now, my daughter, may God go with you. Say ten Hail Marys and light a candle at the shrine of St. Patrick in the crypt. *Absolvo te in nomine Patris, Filii et Spiritus Sancti.*'

Bernadette went home as muddled and torn in her dilemma as she'd been before. Far from going to the police with her dangerous knowledge, she couldn't even bring herself to tell her husband how she'd snooped in Jim's bedroom and found his kitbag full of lethal weapons. The nightmare was still hers alone, and for all the priest's superior wisdom and God-like authority, he'd still fudged the issue and side-stepped a clear-cut decision.

Bernadette had a powerful intuition that if she took action on her own and denounced

Jim Faldo, it would somehow break up their cosy family, and nothing would ever be the same again. Moreover there was the irrational part of her that didn't want anything bad to happen to Jim. Although she kept telling herself that she hated him as a brutal thug, an oppressor of her people over the water, she still liked having him around her in the house. She didn't want him to leave just yet. So she kept quiet and didn't raise the subject any more with Harry about his troublesome brother.

For his part Harry thankfully believed she'd accepted his own easy-going attitude to give Jim the benefit of the doubt, and not hold him responsible for the murder of Ian Melling in Catford. Things would simmer down in time. Jim would be on his way elsewhere without pushing things to a crisis, leaving Harry to mend his clocks and bring up his family in peace.

Then the second brutal Irish murder took place.

# SEVEN

Less than a week after O'Malley's death, Kathleen Donoghue was found dead in London. On a cold, clear night in May, under the yellow blossom of a laburnum tree on Wandsworth Common, she was found just before midnight by a late-night dog-walker on the side of the footpath.

She'd been slashed across the throat by a razor-sharp knife. Both her left and right carotid arteries and her jugular vein had been severed. Exsanguination and death must have occurred in one to three minutes.

Her features were frozen in a grimace of pain and horror. She lay like a slaughtered animal in a coagulating pool of blood. Her long black hair was in disarray and full of dust as she lay convulsed among the casual litter and dog dirt. She hadn't been sexually assaulted, nor had her clothes been disarranged or even touched by the assailant. But perhaps more sinister and revolting than any sex maniac's sick incursion was the disfigurement of her brow: the three letters

IRA carved boldly, deeply and luridly with the point of the murdering knife. The blood had followed the knife, trickling down into her eyes.

Within minutes of the alarm being raised the area was cordoned off by the police, and a canvas shelter was erected over the body for the photographers and medical team to make their preliminary investigation. The high-powered police activity gathered momentum, and a feverish hunt for the murder weapon began as soon as day broke.

The victim's superficial identity was quickly established by the local police, for she'd been resident in Wandsworth for the past two years, working as a receptionist in a small hotel. She called herself Rosyn Fitzgerald, was unmarried and lived in at the Liffey Bridge Hotel. But the terrible graffiti scored on her brow immediately attracted the attention of the Yard's Anti-Terrorist Department. Conferring with the R.U.C. in Belfast, to whom they sent copies of the dead girl's finger-prints, they soon ascertained her true identity as the wanted republican terrorist Kathleen Donoghue, who'd lived quietly in London for years without attracting any attention, except the killer's.

'Well, I reckon that just about wraps it up, guv,' said Detective Sergeant Shindler to the chief inspector. 'Kiernan O'Malley and his poisonous girl friend have been tracked down and eliminated by political hitmen, probably a protestant assassination squad from Belfast. Maybe it's rough justice by our wet standards, but nobody could deny that it's a well earned come-uppance for the two bastards, considering the score in bloodshed and mutilation that's down to them in the past ten years.'

'Fortunately, I'm not responsible for educating you in general morality, Shindler,' said the chief inspector tartly. 'But you know the law, and you're pledged to uphold it. May I remind you that Ian Melling was violently done to death while resident in our manor, so it's down to us to find the assailant. It's just not acceptable to me that some spook should drown a man in his bath, and then walk away unscathed. For all we know it may be some ordinary low-life criminal who went up there to rob him, found he had to kill him to shut him up, and then got in such a panic that he took off without stealing anything.'

'You don't believe that, any more than I do, guv,' retorted Shindler. 'Surely the nasty fate of O'Malley's former girl friend so soon after, with the IRA imprint on her brow means the two killings are connected, probably done by the same organisation for the same political revenge. Besides, the Anti-Terrorist Squad are on the job now, and we'll be duplicating their work. They'll expect to be kept fully informed on anything we turn up, but it'll be one-way traffic. They won't tell us a damned thing, only when they've cleared it up. I reckon we're dead on this case.'

'Do I get the impression that you're less than enthusiastic about this enquiry?' said the chief inspector with a distinct edge to his voice. 'This kind of crime is just plain filthy murder, and I want somebody up the steps for it. If you can't give it all you've got, I'll put somebody else on it. You can go out and find that sneaky skinhead who's been terrorising the old black mammas in the back streets, and nicking their Bingo money.'

'No, that's not necessary, guv,' said Shindler hastily. 'I prefer to stay on the O'Malley murder, even though it is such a challenge. It's negative with all his neighbours, and negative with all the employees in his betting shop. There's nothing from the hostels and doss-houses about strange micks in town, and there's no feed-back from any of the snouts. I reckon the killer was in and out quick without talking to anybody, and was probably on his way back to Belfast before the body was discovered. It belongs with all the other political and sectarian killings over there. Murder is commonplace and it's a flag day when somebody is fingered for it.'

'And the Donoghue girl on Wandsworth Common?'

'Probably the same mob, using a different hit-man with a different technique.'

'Well, you'd better make contact with the Wandsworth C.I.D. and compare notes,' said Sperling grimly. 'See if you can't fumble your way to a common clear-up, because I've got an idea that this is not the end of it. You've drawn blank so far on O'Malley's connections. See if you have better luck with Rosyn Fitzgerald's background. What about that hotel where she worked?'

The Liffey Bridge Hotel was a small family and commercial concern: twelve bedrooms, families and parties catered for; licensed to sell alcoholic beverages; manager Donald

Seamus O'Dowd. It stood in the commercial heart of Wandsworth in a broad but shabby shopping street, with several other more impressive hotels towering over it.

Detective Sergeant Shindler went up the stone steps from pavement to portico and through a heavy glass revolving door into an old-fashioned oak-panelled foyer, where a woman receptionist sat behind a counter in a glassed-in alcove overshadowed by a large Yucca in a jardinière.

This was the manager's wife, Sile O'Dowd, a dark-haired, wiry, intense little woman in her forties, with a plain black dress, a washed-out complexion, and a general drabness which amounted almost to a declaration of war on femininity. She worked an eighteen hour day in the hotel, brought up a large family in her spare time, covered for her lord and master when he was drunk, and tried to be forgiving when he played away.

'Oh, it'll be about Miss Fitzgerald again,' she said, staring from Shindler to his warrant card with bright, black boot-button eyes entirely devoid of warmth. 'Himself will be in the Public Bar as usual.'

Shindler followed her directions down a carpeted passage to a dark, panelled bar-room, reeking of tobacco smoke and hung with horse brasses. There was a large old-fashioned mahogany counter at the far end. As it was out of licensed hours the bar was empty apart from O'Dowd and one of his regular drinking cronies. This was an extremely well fed, pipe-smoking Catholic priest, dressed in black cloak, cape and biretta, who had a tumbler half full of whisky and soda on the glass-topped table before him.

Shindler saw that O'Dowd was fairly well type-cast as an Irish hotelier: a big-bellied, red-faced, hearty man in his fifties, with a few wisps of mouse-coloured hair on his bald dome, and a drooping Mexican bandit's moustache. He laughed a lot and sweated a lot, which accounted for his prodigious thirst. He drank most of the bar profits, but Sile made up for it by her successful management of the hotel's catering side. O'Dowd was a warm, virile, open-handed, sensual man, as all the chippies who'd ever worked in his hotel could happily testify. His features had a crushed, humorous squint, and his sharp grey eyes disappeared in rolls of screwed-up flesh when he laughed.

He was in his shirt sleeves now, and

wreaths of cigar smoke hung about his head from the large fat Havana, which was a part of his genial, free-spending image. But his air of careless geniality was deceptive. O'Dowd was a very shrewd operator with a sharp eye to the hidden snag, the safe short cut, the true cost behind the face value.

Detective Sergeant Shindler introduced himself without preamble, and O'Dowd glanced warily at the warrant card, exchanging a resigned look with the priest.

'I'd like you to tell me all you know about Miss Fitzgerald, who lived in the hotel as one of your employees up to the time of her death.'

'Och, that poor wee girl!' exclaimed the hotelier, his face assuming an expression of deep, concerned sadness. 'What can I say, officer, except that we're all still reeling under the shock? I was never more shattered by grief in my life before, and the good Father will bear me out in that.'

'Aye, I'll certainly do that, Mr. O'Dowd,' nodded the black-cloaked priest gravely, taking a dignified pull at his tumbler, tamping down the tobacco in his pipe bowl. Even indulging in tobacco and alcohol he contrived to look like a pious and abstemious Pope.

'How long had Miss Fitzgerald worked for you here?' said Shindler.

'About two years, and always a good, reliable, well-mannered, clean-living girl, so she was.'

'What do you know of her background, her social life, the people she mixed with in London?'

'I've answered all these questions before, you know, to the Wandsworth police,' grumbled O'Dowd.

'Well, you won't mind going through them again for my benefit,' countered Shindler. 'Do you know who Rosyn Fitzgerald really was?'

'Aye, she comes from a good Catholic family in Andersontown, Belfast, and she came to London two years since to better herself. She was trained as a teacher, but there was no job available for her here, so she came to me as a hotel receptionist, able to do secretarial work. What more can I say?'

'Are you asking me to believe that you had – and still have – no idea of her real identity?'

'Real identity!' exclaimed O'Dowd. 'I'm all at sea, officer. I don't know what you mean. Sure the Wandsworth detectives

74

knew her as Rosyn Fitzgerald, and that's her identity.'

'Well, according to the R.U.C. in Belfast, Rosyn Fitzgerald was really Kathleen Donoghue, a celebrated republican terrorist of the early seventies, wanted for questioning in Belfast, and believed to have been resident in the Irish Republic for the past few years.'

'Great God above!' breathed O'Dowd, his eyes opening wide in shock.

'Did she ever bring any of her men friends to this hotel, or mention anybody she was close to?'

'Indeed she did not. Why would you be asking that?'

'You were her employer and landlord and fellow countryman. If she looked like an innocent, vulnerable girl, I'm sure you must have felt protective towards her. You'd want to keep a watchful eye on her men friends in case she should run into danger.'

'Indeed, and so I would,' declared the hotelier stoutly. 'But she never gave me any cause for alarm along those lines. I already told you, she was a well-behaved, clean-living girl.'

'No camp followers?'

'None whatsoever.'

'Well, she had you fooled,' said Shindler flatly. 'While she was living virtuously in your hotel, she was also associating intimately with another veteran republican, Kiernan O'Malley, over in Catford.'

'I'll not believe it!'

'Please yourself. We found her clothes and her finger-prints in his flat after he was killed. He'd lived here incognito as Ian Melling since seventy-three, and then somebody tracked him down and killed him a few days before the Donoghue/Fitzgerald death. We think the two crimes have a political motive, and are probably closely connected. Which is why I need as much help from you as I can get in reconstructing the girl's activities, both on and off the premises. Her killer may have taken the time and trouble to cultivate her acquaintance and study her habits before he struck.'

'Indeed I'd be only too glad to help you solve this terrible crime,' said O'Dowd fervently. 'But there's nothing I can tell you about Rosyn that you don't know already.'

'Did she ever try to recruit you to her republican cause, or confide in you about her political activities, or ask for your help in advancing them?'

'Indeed she did not!' vowed O'Dowd

indignantly. 'You'll be understanding why I take exception to that insinuation, officer.'

'Granted,' said Shindler graciously. 'What about you then, Father? Did you have any dealings, pastoral or otherwise, with Rosyn Fitzgerald?'

'I regret I never knew the girl. She was not of my flock,' retorted the priest in his soft, rich Irish voice. 'Though I mourn her death no less grievously for that. I've listened to what you had to say to Mr. O'Dowd, and if there's any way I can help you in your investigations, it shall be done, believe me. Such an outcast from humanity should want to get square with God by suffering for his sins, so he should. "Vengeance is mine, saith the Lord".'

'Yes, quite so. I might take you up on that offer, Father, before very long,' said Shindler.

He declined the offer of a requiem drinking session with the two old soaks, and asked O'Dowd for a room to be placed at his disposal where he could interview all the other members of the hotel staff who'd known Rosyn Fitzgerald. The hotelier acceded to his request with alacrity, and as Shindler sat down with notebook and pencil, he reflected that perhaps a close study of the past life and out-of-hours pursuits of Donald O'Dowd might be far more rewarding. The man was altogether too oily and plausible, and if he'd possessed a tail he would have wagged it. Such friendliness towards the police didn't ring true in Shindler's ear, especially from a Republican Irishman who'd given bed and board for over two years to Kathleen Donoghue, and still maintained he didn't know who she really was.

## EIGHT

To Harry Faldo in Camberwell, news of the second murder brought an even greater trauma than the first. In the evening paper the savage killing of Rosyn Fitzgerald on Wandsworth Common was described in all its gruesome detail. It stirred up far more newspaper prominence and passion than the Melling murder because it had the elements that the media ghouls really love: The victim was an attractive young woman brutally cut down in her prime; the bestial disfigurement invoked the Irish dimension in London, and brought it into the open where nobody could fudge the issue. It prompted excited speculation by feature writers as to whether Rosyn Fitzgerald actually had some past involvement on one side or the other with the tribal terrorism.

Harry Faldo read the prominent paragraph, and the blood slowly drained from his face.

'Oh, my God!' he groaned. 'This is awful. It was stupid as well as barbarous. Marking her like that, it's bound to start the backlash.'

'Backlash? What are you talking about?' cried Bernadette, vigorously powdering the baby's bottom. 'What's happened? Are you all right?'

He gave her the evening paper, and lowered himself into a chair, putting his head in his hands.

'Rosyn Fitzgerald is an Irish name. I'll bet all the money I've got it was an alias for Kathleen Donoghue. Jim must have found her like he said he would. He forced O'Malley to tell him where she was.'

'Holy-Mary-Mother-of-God!' exclaimed Bernadette hysterically. 'You mean to tell me you knew all along this was going to happen, and you just did nothing! You sheltered that bloodthirsty bastard upstairs while he was plotting another bloody murder! You're as guilty as he is. Well, that's the finish of it, Harry Faldo. You get rid of that brotherly thug of yours now, today, or I'm going to the poliss to tell them everything. So help me God!'

'What's this about going to the police?' said Jim Faldo who'd suddenly appeared in the doorway, having come down for his tea. He was dressed casually in khaki drill slacks, plaid shirt and canvas sneakers, and as always he moved in swift-footed silence.

'It's about this,' said Bernadette fiercely, pointing to the announcement of the Wandsworth Common murder. 'You did it, didn't you? It's part of your bloody feuding across the water, so it is. You told Harry you'd come to London to kill a Republican girl.'

'What are you getting so steamed up about?' said Jim coolly. 'You're jumping to conclusions again. In any case she was just a bloody bog-bred ball-breaker who lived ten years too long.'

'I warned you the first day you came here. "None of your war games here", I said, because I knew you, Jim Faldo.'

'Did you hear me last night, coming or

going, on those bloody creaking stairs?'

'No, but that doesn't mean a damned thing. People like you walk through walls and climb over roofs, so they do.'

'The police will be very impressed with that as evidence,' sneered Jim.

'That's as maybe. But they'll certainly be impressed with that sackful of guns and bombs you're keeping up there in your wardrobe. Enough to start a war, so there is.'

The mocking smile vanished from his lips, and his mood became cold and deadly.

'So you've been snooping about among my belongings, you nosey bitch! I should have known it. It was a bad mistake to come here. Who have you told about me?'

'Nobody,' she gasped, frightened by the intensity of his anger.

'Who?' he shouted, grabbing her by the arms and shaking her till her teeth rattled.

'Well, only the Father at St. Patrick's Church,' she stammered. 'I had to go to confession, and it all came pouring out: how you'd come here threatening murder to the Republicans, and how you'd got enough weapons for your own private army. I didn't know what to do. I had to tell the Father.'

'You fool!' he raged. 'You bloody priest-ridden, treacherous fool. You've sold me to the enemy.'

'No!' she cried as he flung her aside. 'The Father would never repeat anything heard at confession. It's as safe as telling it to God.'

'Like hell it is! Every bloody Catholic, priest or layman, they're all in on the conspiracy. And even if they're not, how do you know the hard men haven't got every priest's house and confession box bugged? Well, you've got your wish. I'll be out of here within an hour. I'd be asking for it, a sitting duck, now you've blabbed it all in a confession box.'

'But where will you go?' said Harry, pale and distressed by the scene.

'Anywhere. The sewers would be safer.'

'Shall we be seeing you again?'

'I doubt it. I was a bloody fool even to consider coming here with you married to one of the enemy. You'd better watch it, Harry. She's a mick first and a wife second. If she ever has to make the choice she'll drop you in it, kids and all.'

# NINE

A couple of days after the murder of Rosyn Fitzgerald, Detective Chief Inspector Sperling received a confidential memo from the Anti-Terrorist Squad at the Yard, and he lost no time in passing it on to Detective Sergeant Shindler.

'There's been a warning from the R.U.C. in Belfast,' he said. 'They have intelligence reports from a usually reliable source that two top killers from the Provisional I.R.A. have set out for London from Belfast.'

'Oh, that's bloody marvellous!' exclaimed Shindler in disgust. 'Can't they be picked up as soon as they land?'

'Naturally there'll be a sharp watch kept by Special Branch on all the ports and airfields. But we don't know who they are. No names have been given. So they've only got to go down to Dublin and come in here as bona fide citizens of the Republic.'

'Of course. What could be easier? This is a very wet country,' declared Shindler, 'and I'm not talking about the rainfall either.

Hasn't the R.U.C. heard from its reliable source what the two goons are coming here for?'

'They don't know that. But it doesn't need much working out that they're coming here to kill somebody.'

'They're not getting dug in for the Royal Wedding in a couple of months time, are they?'

'Possibly but highly unlikely,' replied the chief inspector. 'They only go for soft targets. Security's going to be so tight round St. Paul's on the big day that nothing less than an air strike could manage to hit the principal targets. It would certainly take more than a couple of village butchers to bring that off and they know it, so they won't even try.'

'What do you reckon they're after then, guv?'

'I've got a very strong gut feeling that it's something to do with those recent Irish killings here and on Wandsworth Common,' replied Sperling. 'The Provos must know something that we don't, like who did those killings and the fact that he's still in London. We know they have a pretty good track record for looking after their own, and Kiernan O'Malley was a real Republican hero. They won't let him be put down without a bloodthirsty counter stroke.'

'So it is turning into an Irish vendetta on the London streets, guv, like you said. How the hell can they know who did it, over in Belfast, when we're here on the spot and can't find a single lead?'

'It's the same with all secret terror organisations. They've got a wide network of narks and snouts, and they get things done in the dark. A rule of terror, with knee-caps shot off, bodies in the river, and men hung up on meat hooks is bound to give them a head start over us. We'll just have to stand by and wait for something to happen so that we can react to it. Have you completed interviews with all the people who had anything to do with Rosyn Fitzgerald?'

'Yes, guv. I'm getting the reports typed out now. The only man of real interest among her associates was her employer who runs the Liffey Bridge Hotel, Donald Seamus O'Dowd. So I thought I'd have some research done into his past history and present activities.'

'And what did you get out of that?' said the chief inspector curiously.

'O'Dowd is fifty-six years old and his roots are in Southern Ireland, County Kilkenny.

He came over here in the war, nineteen forty-two, and joined the R.A.F. ground staff as an engine fitter. With his blarney and bullshit he was soon a sergeant, and spent a cosy war on a bomber station at Scampton in Lincolnshire, leaning up against an engine in a hangar and doing all the work with his mouth.

'When the war ended they took the engine away from him, so he came to London and went into the hotel business. He married a fellow countrywoman who also worked in hotels, and they went into hotel management together. O'Dowd never made any secret of his Republican sympathies, and he used to join in all the protest marches and demonstrations. He had I.R.A. collection boxes stuck all over his hotel.

'When the Price sisters and their goons came over in seventy-three to bomb the law courts, one of their squad left a strong trail to the Liffey Bridge. So O'Dowd had a very rough time from the Bomb Squad and Special Branch. But there wasn't enough evidence to prove his complicity, so they left him out. Then when they brought in the Prevention of Terrorism Act, and he realised he could be deported at short notice if he stuck his neck out too far, he knew he had to cut out all his overt support for the I.R.A. and keep a low profile. He probably still donates what he can afford to the cause, and helps behind the scenes with their fund-raising. But the Wandsworth police have watched him pretty carefully since the Price sisters' carnival hit town, and they're satisfied he's not into anything heavy.

'O'Dowd never leaves his hotel except for a day at the races or a tour round the golf course to the nineteenth hole. He doesn't harbour low-life thugs or terrorist suspects in his hotel. All his staff are fellow country-men and women, but they've all been investigated and passed as harmless. Rosyn Fitzgerald was the only employee with a past, and according to the other loyal workers, O'Dowd's interest in her was more sexual than political. She had very privi-leged status there, and certainly did a lot more for him than lick his stamps. O'Dowd's wife didn't like it a bit.'

'Did you get the impression that O'Dowd knew more about O'Malley and Donoghue than he was prepared to admit?'

'That was my gut feeling, though he went out of his way to convince me how much he loves England, and he thinks our police over here are wonderful. According to several of his workers, he broke down and wept when the police came to tell him what had happened to Rosyn Fitzgerald, and didn't sober up for the rest of the day.'

'Well, I suppose that could mean his heart's in the right place,' commented the chief inspector. 'But warm, emotional men are often emotional about the wrong things. It might not be a bad idea to keep an eye on O'Dowd and his hotel for the next week or two, just in case the two hit men from Belfast should use the Liffey Bridge as a staging post while they're seeking out whoever it is they've come to kill.'

'I'll see to it, guv. But I wouldn't have thought they'd risk shacking up with O'Dowd now his cover's blown.'

'Well, go on keeping your ear to the ground among the cheap hotels and doss houses. Check on the D.H.S.S. offices as well. The two visitors might have arranged to collect their Social Security money here instead of Belfast, while they're setting up the kill.'

'A very wet country,' grumbled Shindler morosely as he went out.

# TEN

The two killers flew into London airport on a scheduled Aer Lingus flight from Dublin. They had impeccable credentials as salesmen: one to promote the sales of quartz kitchen clocks manufactured by a Japanese company in Wexford; the other to push a new line in Irish linen tea towels, colourfully imprinted with historical insignia, pageantry and coats of arms for the forthcoming royal wedding.

They travelled separately in different seats in the aircraft, and ignored each other like total strangers. The last impression they wanted to give the watching Special Branch men at the air terminal was that they were together as a team.

The senior assassin was Sean Mooney from the Bogside, aged thirty-five, five feet six inches tall and running to fat, a man born and bred for violence. His large pale eyes gave him the look of a lazy bull-frog. He had a bald head and a pear-shaped, amiable face with a ready, humorous smile.

In his new well-cut raincoat and soft felt hat he was an innocuous, indeterminate figure which could merge inconspicuously into a company of three. He gave not the slightest hint of villainy, or the shadowed paranoia of one who'd lived with violence for most of his life. His body count so far was twenty-one Brits, and he had every hope of notching up the century before the map of Ireland was coloured all in green. Then he'd have to content himself with knocking off suspected Orange men, ex-policemen and other Protestant enemies of the State.

His junior and second string was Kevin Royle from the New Lodge area of Belfast, ten years younger and not so cunning or accomplished as Mooney in killing from ambush, but moving up fast with growing confidence and growing deadliness. His body count was only seven Brits and five off-duty policemen so far, but he was young, and the world was all before him. He looked clean and smartly dressed, with the stance of an athlete and the clean-cut, earnest face of a choir boy. It was obvious that he was going to make a real hit with his new line in Royal Souvenir Irish linen, just as the royal wedding euphoria was rising to its mushiest.

With the fifty-odd equally innocuous looking other passengers they trooped off the tarmac to Terminal 2 Arrivals, passed through the airport building after no more than a perfunctory glance from work-to-rule customs officers, and out to the waiting ranks of taxis. Still not acknowledging each other's existence, they took separate cabs for Waterloo Station, and finally got together over a drink in the station buffet. Then they proceeded by Underground to the safe house in Walworth, where bed and board had been arranged for them as long as they should need it.

Their host was Thomas McClusky, driver for a security firm, who'd lived peacefully in London with his wife Maya for more than twenty years. He'd almost forgotten what Ireland looked like, and his Irish accent was now barely noticeable. He was an integrated Londoner, but when the call came from London Sinn Fein to help out a couple of business men from across the water in need of accommodation and privacy, he responded without question like a trained seal. He would never be told what they were there for, and he had more sense than to ask.

The assassins had been given the single

name, Faldo of Camberwell, by their Intelligence branch, and, more significantly, the fact that he was S.A.S. Membership of the S.A.S. brought instant sentence of death by the I.R.A. The Regiment's soldiers and ex-soldiers were to be hunted down and exterminated wherever they showed themselves in any part of the world. It was a major priority. In addition to this Faldo being S.A.S., the word had come from a very reliable source that he was also responsible for the London murders of the veteran patriot Kiernan O'Malley, and the brave, affectionately regarded girl soldier, Kathleen Donoghue.

As soon as they'd checked into the McClusky house, they changed into their jeans, leather jackets and sneakers, the usual anonymous uniform of urban guerrillas, and went mooching about the streets of Camberwell, unnoticed among all the other drop-outs. Casual enquiry elicited the fact that there was only one Faldo in Camberwell, the man who sold old clocks. He was in his late twenties and had been in the British Army. (That was good enough!) But he'd been discharged on medical grounds, and had married an Irish girl from Belfast. (Another bloody good reason to take him out.)

They had no trouble locating Harry Faldo's shop in its dismal, run-down street. They walked all round it with a superficial tactical reconnaissance, and went back to Walworth to enjoy the good plain cooking of Maya McClusky.

Their first operational move was to steal a car, the inevitable Ford Cortina which was fast, easy to drive and anonymous because of its vast numbers on the London streets. Once they were mobile they set out to pick up their weapons, a Sterling sub-machine gun and a Browning automatic pistol apiece from a backstreet garage in Kilburn, that was legally and inconspicuously operated by a former I.R.A. man, and served as the Provisionals' armoury for London operations.

At dead of night the killers arrived quietly in the deserted, poorly lit street, parked their car on a strip of waste ground without slamming any doors, and moved in towards Harry Faldo's shop. In the distance some church clock struck one. A goods train rattled by on the viaduct, and a cold night wind blew from the direction of the Thames.

Mooney and Royle went in through the shop's back yard where Harry Faldo kept his invalid car, and jemmied open the back door that led into a store and work room. By the light of an electric torch they swarmed frenziedly down the passage, glancing quickly in each ground floor room to make sure they were unoccupied. So tense and wound up that they were ready to explode, they rushed up the stairs to the living quarters on the first floor. Doors banged as they hurtled in and out of rooms in a wild panic to get the job done fast and then get far away.

Harry Faldo who was a light sleeper had been wakened by the sudden crack of the back door bursting open. He listened in alarm to the other noises, and then broke out in a cold sweat as he realised intruders were in the house. He struggled to sit upright in the bed and reached for his walking sticks. His frantic movements awoke Bernadette who slept heavily.

'What's the matter?' she grumbled irritably. 'It's a terrible bloody fidget you are.'

'There's somebody in the house,' whispered Harry. 'Listen!'

As he switched the bedside light on there came the crash of a door being shut down below, and then the rapid thud of footsteps on the creaking stairs.

'Holy Mary!' gasped Bernadette in terror. 'It's burglars to be sure. Get to the telephone and call the poliss.'

Unfortunately the only telephone on that floor was in the living room, and the pounding crescendo of footsteps on the stairs told Harry that he'd never make it. He'd just managed to stagger upright on his feet when the door flew open and the killers burst in, one behind the other, with sub-machine guns held at hip level. They were a horrible nightmare spectacle in their Balaclava helmets and zipped-up leather jackets, with their cold, psychopaths' eyes, and their mouths tightly clenched in the high, adrenaline-charged tension of their trade.

'Are you Faldo?' snarled the thick-set, jowly man.

'Yes,' gasped Harry.

'S.A.S.?'

'No! Not me!'

'F-ing lying git!' shouted Mooney, and pressed the trigger of his sub-machine gun.

Instantly the room was filled with un-bearable noise, the harsh, penetrating clatter of the rapid-firing weapon, and the mind-less, hysterical screams of Bernadette. Chips of plaster flew off the wall behind him as Harry was stitched up tight across the chest with a line of machine gun bullets, and hurled backwards across the bed. Bernadette's screams were cut off in a choking gurgle as the weapon was turned on her with another burst. Then there was an appalling silence and a stillness on the bloodstained bed. The room was full of choking cordite fumes and the smell of warm blood.

'Don't just bloody stand there,' snarled Mooney to his twitching back-up man. 'Get over the rest of the bloody house and make sure there's no other S.A.S. bastard here. We could be in a real bloody ambush here, for Christ's sake!'

Kevin Royle burst into the next bedroom where the three baby boys were sound asleep in their cots, so far undisturbed by all the commotion. The gunman shone his torch on them, and for a single heady moment his finger trembled on the trigger as his Sterling hovered over the three cots. Then he shrugged, and the high tension went out of him as he dimly realised there was no glory to be had, even in his mob, for shooting babies in their beds.

'Jesus! They're only f-ing weans!' he

muttered as he shut the door on them and burst into Jim Faldo's former room. He looked under the bed and inside the empty wardrobe. Having made sure that the rest of the house and shop was unoccupied, the assassins made their escape quickly the way they had come. They jumped into their Cortina and roared away with screeching tyres towards the Thames and Kilburn, where they returned their weapons to the Provisionals' armoury. Then they dumped the car in a street lined with other parked cars, and returned the last half mile on foot to the McClusky house in Walworth.

Mission accomplished! They were booked on the early morning flight out of Heathrow, and with average luck they would be back in Dublin before the Camberwell killings were even discovered.


## ELEVEN

On the day of the Faldo funerals the mourners filled the small memorial chapel in the South London cemetery. They were nearly all poor people, black and white, from the twilight neighbourhood in Camberwell, for Harry and Bernadette had been well liked among the local community.

Everybody was stunned with horror at the meaningless and motiveless bestiality of the dual killing. Why had terrorists made such a big production over killing a poor harmless cripple and his wife? The police had their own theories about the reasons for the atrocity, but they were keeping very tight-lipped about it, and refused all comment to the press until they had something more positive to work on.

Far from being the usual funeral weather, with the rain and the low, weeping clouds contributing to the oppression of everybody's spirits, it was a glorious summer's day with tulips in bloom round the well kept graves, and masses of pink blossom on the ornamental trees waving in the sunshine.

Among the representatives from the police were Detective Sergeant Shindler and Detective Constable Neilson who were still hoping for a lead on the murder of Ian Melling. Shindler had a camera with a zoom lens suspended on a strap round his neck, and every now and again he would take a quick snap of some face among the mourners whom he fancied as a likely customer for police attention. Both detectives were keeping an incessant sharp-eyed watch on the gathering in case there was some furtive interloper, some stranger from the wrong side of the tracks, or some gruesome human outcast who might be there with a more pronounced interest than the usual ghoulish curiosity in a double interment.

At the brief ritual round the open grave, as the befrocked clergyman intoned his solemn litany, Shindler's interest suddenly fastened on a man standing at the graveside, staring dry-eyed with a face like thunder at the two coffins. He was casually dressed in old threadbare denims, lumberjack's shirt and donkey jacket. But Shindler knew instinctively that he was no mere idle loafer or ghoulish participant in other men's griefs. His trim, taut and trained physique and general bearing looked out of character with his hippy-style pose as a drop-out. Compared with the rest of the congregation he was a complete outsider. The way he kept clenching and unclenching his hands showed that he was possessed by some violent and repressed feeling as he watched the coffins sink slowly out of sight and heard the clatter of the symbolic earth thrown down on their lids.

Shindler took a couple of snaps of him, one full face and one in profile as for C.R.O. records.

When the last tribute had been paid, and the grim-faced neighbours with their tearful women had all dispersed, Shindler and Neilson followed the interesting stranger out of the cemetery to find out more about him. If he was some close friend or relative of the Faldos, he might have some knowledge of the reason behind their brutal murder.

Without seeming to know or care that he was being followed, their quarry walked unhurriedly along Brockley Way and turned into a large Victorian pub called The Blue Anchor. In the public bar he ordered a pint of bitter and when to sit down alone and morose at a circular bar table in an empty alcove. Presently Shindler and Neilson, each carrying a pint, came strolling over and sat on the banquette, one on each side of him, setting their drinks down on his table. He glanced at them warily and his muscles tightened, ready for anything.

'Mind if we join you?' said Shindler jocularly. 'We noticed you over in the cemetery at the funeral of the young couple.

Relations of yours, were they, or just neighbours?'

The cold greenish eyes of the stranger considered him speculatively, noting the air of authority and the heavy, ape-like physique of Shindler.

At length he said: 'What the bloody hell business is it of yours?'

Shindler sighed resignedly and produced his warrant card.

'C.I.D.,' he explained. 'We have an interest when a harmless man and wife get murdered in their beds by bloody maniacs.'

'Oh, yes? Well, why don't you get on your bikes and find those bloody maniacs?'

'What else do you think we're doing, spending time with you?' retorted Shindler tartly.

'You don't think I killed them, do you, and then went to their funeral to gloat?'

'What was your interest in those two people? Presumably you knew them, or you wouldn't have been at their funeral.'

'Oh, I just knew Faldo as a shopkeeper,' he replied. 'I bought a clock off him once.'

'You wouldn't call them intimate friends of yours?'

'Not at all.'

'Well, the way I read it,' said Shindler

bluntly, 'you looked really upset and ready to blow your cool when you were standing at that graveside. It was more as if the victims were close friends than a tradesman and his wife who once flogged you a clock.'

'I don't deny I was upset. Pointless killing and bereavement always turns me up. Besides, I was thinking of three baby boys who'll grow up unloved, kicked about from hell to breakfast, warped and mixed up by the bureaucratic do-gooders of the Welfare State.'

'I see,' said Shindler, staring at him thoughtfully. 'What did you say your name was, Mr – er–?'

'I didn't.'

'Well, who are you then? You have a name, presumably, or do you have a reason for keeping it from us?'

'Norcross. John Norcross.'

'Occupation?'

'Unemployed at present.'

'What were you when you did work?'

'Motor mechanic.'

'Your address?'

'You could say I'm between digs at present.'

'No fixed abode,' nodded Shindler. 'So why did you buy an old clock from Harry

102

Faldo? Not exactly the sort of portable thing to lug around digs, hostels and flophouses, was it?'

'I had a place of my own when I bought the clock, and my own things around me,' snapped Norcross. 'I wasn't always an unemployed jerk.'

'Well, I think you're a bit of a mystery man, Mr. Norcross,' said Shindler, 'and I don't think you've been completely frank with us. There are certain inconsistencies in your account of yourself and your presence at the Faldo funeral that I'd like properly cleared up. So would you have any objection to coming with us to the Station to get a few things straightened out?'

'What the bloody hell can I tell you at the Station that I haven't told you already?' demanded Norcross, bristling with hostility.

'I'd just like you to meet my guv'nor,' said Shindler conciliatingly. 'He's interested in eccentrics who go to funerals for kicks.'

'My God!' exclaimed Norcross bitterly. 'You cozzers may be on the run from the criminals and the blacks and the demo men, but you certainly know how to sock it to poor harmless buggers like me who haven't got a union. What are you arresting me for? Is it a crime to go to a bloody funeral?'

'Oh, this is not an arrest,' said Shindler jovially. 'Just something in the nature of getting to know you. If you refuse to come in for a peaceful chat with the guv'nor, we shall obviously start thinking you've got something to hide. It might mean surveillance and extensive enquiries as to what you've been up to for most of your life. But if you come like an innocent citizen you'll be clean with us. You might even get a cup of tea and your dinner out of it, and what have you got to lose but time, that you've got too much of anyway?'

Detective Constable Neilson, who'd been watching the man closely, had an uneasy feeling that he was going to break out, go berserk like any man of violence who finds himself in an unacceptable situation. In fact Neilson had a long moment of real anxiety as their customer considered Shindler's proposition, for he was experienced enough to know that this joker could give a good account of himself if he decided to make the detectives earn their money.

'Go back to the cemetery, Frank, and fetch the car,' said Shindler, 'while I buy Mr. Norcross another pint.'

Norcross eventually allowed them to drive him to the police station peacefully enough, and he was ushered into an interview room to wait, while Shindler went off to explain the situation to Detective Chief Inspector Sperling. The latter was immediately interested in the suspicious looking stranger who'd been noticed at the graveside and brought in for questioning.

'This is quite a turn-up,' said Sperling, 'in view of what I've just been told by Chief Superintendent Scantlebury of the Anti-Terrorist Squad. They've looked into the background of this Harry Faldo of Camberwell. It seems he's an ex-member of the British Army, and served in Ulster until he was invalided out.'

'Ah,' said Shindler resignedly. 'The Irish connection again!'

'Apparently he was shot up in a particularly nasty I.R.A. ambush and left for dead. He survived by a miracle, but was left a permanent cripple, just able to stagger around with a couple of sticks. Some time after his discharge, when he'd set himself up as a clockmaker, he went back to Belfast and married the Catholic nurse who'd looked after him in the Royal Victoria.'

'It seems a bit heavy, even for that lot, for the I.R.A. to follow him over here and kill him just for that,' observed Shindler.

The chief inspector shook his head reprovingly.

'You're jumping the gun again, Shindler. That's not it at all. The Anti-Terrorist Squad have got the file on Faldo from the Ministry of Defence Records. Harry Faldo had an older brother, James Montgomery Faldo, his only surviving relative. This one's a hard case, a regular soldier all his life, in the Parachute Regiment and recently in the S.A.S. He's proficient in the martial arts, a Sixth Dan at Karate. He served out his time and got his discharge on April the thirtieth, and his former commanding officer thinks he was on his way to London to visit his brother Harry.'

'That's it then, guv,' said Shindler with a sudden inspiration. 'The I.R.A. hit squad who murdered Harry Faldo were really after his brother, the S.A.S. man.'

'It seems a logical explanation,' conceded the chief inspector cautiously. 'With their usual sloppy intelligence work, and bloodthirsty eagerness to make a score, they found the name Faldo in Camberwell, established that he was a former serving soldier in the British Army, and didn't stop to find out that he was only the harmless younger brother. Which brings us to that interesting stranger you've just picked up at the Faldos' funeral. Mr. Norcross, isn't it?'

'Good God!' exclaimed Shindler all agog. 'You think this joker could really be the brother, the hard case S.A.S. man who the micks were really after?'

'Don't you think so?'

'Of course. No wonder he went to the funeral, and looked so pissed off at the graveside. But why did he give us a false name?'

'We'll have to ask him, won't we?' said the chief inspector, getting up from his desk. 'Lead on, Sergeant.'

As they walked into the interview room and dismissed the supervising constable, the stranger was pacing up and down like a caged animal.

'About bloody time, too,' he growled. 'Say what you have to say, and get me out of here.'

'Sit down, Mr. Norcross,' said the chief inspector amiably, indicating a plain straight-backed chair. 'I'm Detective Chief Inspector Sperling. My sergeant tells me he noticed you at the Faldo funeral over in Camberwell New Cemetery.'

'And was I behaving suspiciously? Did he tell you I was picking pockets?'

'Why were you at the funeral, Mr. Norcross?'

'I've already told him,' replied the stranger, gesturing contemptuously at Shindler. 'And why haven't you brought in all the other nosey buggers at that funeral? Why pick on me?'

'Why did you give my sergeant a false name when he spoke to you? What were you trying to hide?'

'Why would I give him a false name?' countered the other defiantly. 'I told him my name, John Norcross.'

'Stop wasting my time!' snapped the chief inspector harshly. 'Your name is James Montgomery Faldo. You've recently been discharged from the British Army in Northern Ireland, where you were a sergeant in the S.A.S. Regiment. True or false?'

Taken by surprise, the man stared at him in shocked incredulity.

'Come on, there's no point in being coy about it,' persisted Sperling relentlessly. 'We can easily get a photograph and all the necessary specifications about you from Ministry of Defence records. If necessary we can get an officer down from your regiment to identify you. Why did you try to conceal your real identity from the police?'

For a moment the other was silent, glowering at the chief inspector. Then he said, 'All right. I'm Faldo. As to why I want to be incognito here, isn't it bloody obvious after what they've done to my brother? That shoot-out was meant for me, you know. But they're so bloody incompetent they killed the first Faldo they could find.'

'Why was it meant for you?'

'Oh, for Christ's sake!' exclaimed Faldo in disgust. 'Don't you know anything? It's because I'm S.A.S. Those I.R.A. micks are paranoid about us over there. As soon as their hard men hear the S.A.S. has moved in on any operation, they wet their pants and scuttle off into the Republic for a good long rest. But they get their own back by marking us down wherever we show up on our own. Any former S.A.S. man who hangs his sign up anywhere in the world can expect a visit from those bastards.'

'So knowing that, why did you visit your brother in Camberwell and draw them down on him?'

'How was I to know they'd be on to me so fast? I was on leave in London, and he was my only relative. It seemed safe enough to spend a week with him. How the hell did they know there was a Faldo in Camberwell?'

'That's a very good question,' said Sperling. 'There are some aspects of this case that completely baffle me. For one thing, there must be dozens of S.A.S. men who serve out their time and go their own separate ways afterwards without getting their relatives slaughtered by the I.R.A. So what's so special about you, Faldo, that brings them down on your family within a week or two of your leaving the Regiment?'

'I've no idea,' replied Faldo warily. 'I've always done my job wherever I've been sent, but never gone out of my way to be a sadist or a gung-ho mick exterminator like some I could mention.'

The chief inspector considered him thoughtfully for a time.

'You see,' he continued, 'about a week before your brother's house was attacked, we received a tip-off from the R.U.C. in Belfast that a top I.R.A. murder squad had set out for London. We didn't know why they were coming, or anything about their intended targets. We didn't even know the Faldos existed until they were suddenly front-page news as the victims of a terrorist attack. So the question now arises, how did the I.R.A. far away in Belfast know about the Faldos? Why had you been marked down for such special treatment, just a soldier doing his job? Did you get into something over your head?'

'I haven't a clue,' replied Faldo flatly.

'You were discharged from the army at Army H.Q. at Lisburn in Northern Ireland on April the thirtieth. When did you arrive in London?'

'A couple of days later, May the second, I suppose.'

'And you went straight to your brother's house in Camberwell?'

'That's right.'

'You say you'd come to visit him for a spell. So where were you on the night of the twenty-fifth when the terrorists struck?'

'I'd moved out by then. I only stayed about a couple of weeks. I didn't want to impose on them indefinitely. Bernadette – she had her work cut out with a young family.'

'I see,' said the chief inspector thoughtfully. 'And where are you living now?'

'Some nights I go to a spike, a Salvation Army Hostel or Council Home for the unemployed and homeless. For one pound twenty you can get a bed for the night. If it's warm I kip down in the open in a park or public garden. It's a good deal fresher and cleaner and less dangerous than a spike.'

'What do you mean? How is it less dangerous?'

'Most of the bums in those places are alcoholics,' replied Faldo, 'and as they can't afford whisky they're on the meths. One night I spent in a Council Home for working men over in Lambeth, I was woken up at two o'clock by a lousy drunken jock punching me in the face and saying I'd pinched his bed. When I gave him an argument he started to puke all over me. It was fresher smelling among the dustbins where I spent the rest of the night.'

'Yes, well, are you so short of funds that you can't go to a cheap, clean hotel or bed-and-breakfast place?'

'I might afford it,' retorted Faldo, 'but I'm not sure I'd be all that safe. I'd be trapped there like a rat in a hole if those bloody micks should flush me out. But in a hostel among the human derelicts, forty or fifty bodies in a stinking dormitory, not even the I.R.A. are likely to come in and shoot the bloody lot in the hope of nailing Faldo.'

'And what are your plans for the future?'

'Don't worry. I won't be a problem to you,' replied Faldo. 'You won't have to sweep me up off the street and fill in the report for a Coroner's inquest.'

'That's not what I asked,' said Sperling. 'Are you staying on in civilian life now you're paid off, or will you sign on again?'

'I hadn't given it much thought, what with everything else that's come down on me just lately. But I might try being respectable if there are any decent civvie jobs going.'

'All right, Mr. Faldo,' sighed the chief inspector. 'That'll be all. You can go now. But keep your nose clean. Don't even consider any idea of revenge for what's happened. No setting yourself up as a private army, fighting that old war that you've just got out of.'

'As if I would!' said Faldo with an air of self-righteous innocence. 'I don't even possess a chiv to my name!'

## TWELVE

As soon as the ex-soldier had gone, Sperling said thoughtfully: 'That was a funny remark to make for an ex-S.A.S. man, trained in every conceivable form of weaponry: "I don't even possess a chiv." Why would he want us to know that he doesn't own a knife?'

'Maybe you're way ahead of him, guv,' shrugged Shindler. 'A ten-year-old can go in any sports shop or ironmonger's and buy a cheap serviceable knife of any shape or size, that's an instant deadly weapon. If Faldo needs a knife, he'll get one at the corner shop.'

'I know,' said the chief inspector, 'but it still seems a bit odd calling our attention to it. Get a man to follow him, find out where he goes and what he's up to. He looks as if he could be a pretty dangerous customer, and he's just had a hell of an experience to get steamed up about. I don't want him taking the law into his own hands and knocking off a few of our resident London Irish.'

'O.K., guv. Neilson's seen him face to face. I'll get him to keep an eye on our desperado.'

Next day however, Shindler had to come to the chief inspector to report that his man had failed in his mission.

'Sorry, guv,' he said ruefully. 'We've lost Faldo.'

'How?'

'Normally Neilson's pretty good at sur-

114

veillance. He managed to stay with Faldo all day yesterday, in and out of the pubs and betting shops, feeding the ducks in the park, even a half-hour visit to a cat-house to get laid by a spade. But Faldo must have sussed our hero and was stringing him along. At nine o'clock last night he checked into Bennett House. That's a hostel for destitute men run by the Council in Lambeth, a big Victorian building that used to be local government offices.

'Neilson checked in as well and hired a bed for one pound twenty, just to make sure Faldo was safely bedded and he knew where he was. But Faldo got lost somehow among all those drunks and derelicts. The bed he hired wasn't slept in. The Superintendent didn't see him come down the main staircase. While Neilson thought he was in the toilets he must have been climbing out through a window and down an outlet pipe two floors up. Anyhow he's clean away, and it makes you wonder why he'd risk his neck to give us the slip if he wasn't up to something.'

'Don't worry about it,' said Sperling. 'It may be just a phobia of his, an insecure man's hostility to somebody with big feet trailing round after him. If he gets up to anything indictable we'll pull him in fast enough.'

'There's something else about him, guv,' said Shindler. 'Something that we missed out on at the time because we didn't know anything about the Faldos.'

'Oh? What, for instance?"

'I've been looking again through all those statements taken from local residents and neighbours in Lewisham Park district immediately after the murder of Melling/O'Malley.'

The chief inspector put his pen down and looked at Shindler intently.

'Go on.'

'There's a cantankerous old dowager, Mrs. Clare Emmet-Viger, who lives down the road a couple of hundred yards from Melling's block, in a big old house that she's had converted into flats. She's a very poor sleeper and gets up at all hours to make tea, paint pictures, and play her Ouija Board. On the night when Melling was killed she looked out of her front window at about one a.m., and saw one of those motorised, three-wheeled invalid carriages parked at the kerb slap outside her house when she'd thought it was clear for the night.

'Mrs. Emmet-Viger has a phobia about

cars making the road look untidy outside her window, so that she has to sit and look at a line of ugly old scrap iron. She has numerous up-and-downers and fights long running battles with car owners who come and park outside her house during the day, as if she owns the road as well as the house. She's even been known to go out there and fling buckets of dirty water all over them, until she was had up for causing a breach of the peace.'

'How is this relevant to Faldo?' said the chief inspector patiently.

'I was interested in her description of the three-wheeled invalid car that she'd never seen before. So I went and had a look at the slum shop in Camberwell where the two Faldos were shot to death. And would you believe it, guv! In the yard at the back there was one of those little cripple buggies that used to be supplied by the N.H.S. to improve the mobility of the disabled. Harry Faldo had one because he was crippled in Ireland. Coincidence, guv, or where does it leave us if this should be the same vehicle that was parked a couple of hundred yards from O'Malley's flat at the time he was killed?'

'I see what you mean,' said Sperling

quickly, reaching for his diary. 'Let's check the time scheme. On May the second James Faldo arrived in London to stay with his brother. Just over a week later on May the tenth, Kiernan O'Malley was drowned in his bath by a violent intruder. Five days later the I.R.A. girl Rosyn Fitzgerald had her throat cut on Wandsworth Common, and the letters IRA carved on her brow. (Faldo was at pains to inform us when we had him in that he doesn't even own a knife). On May the eighteenth we received that tip-off from the R.U.C. that a top I.R.A. murder team was thought to have set out from Belfast for London. One week later, on May the twenty-fifth, Harry Faldo and his wife were murdered in their beds by the hit squad, which we can only assume to be the assassination team we were warned about. Somehow – God only knows how – the Irish grapevine here got a lead on Faldo as the liquidator, and called in their heavy mob.

'As soon as he'd completed his bloody assignment Faldo moved out of his brother's house to go on his way, not realising or not caring that he'd brought down murderers from the other side on his innocent relatives. Yes, it hangs together perfectly well chronologically, and I want some answers from Mr. Faldo. Put out a call to have James Faldo picked up for questioning on suspicion of murder. I've got an awful feeling that we could be into shrink territory with this one.'

## THIRTEEN

Father Niall Daniel Fogarty-Fegan of St. Patrick's, Camberwell was a plump, pink, sleek man in his fifties. A tonsure of greying hair surrounded his high bald dome, which he kept covered at all times with his biretta. His earthly cares were food and drink, and he laughed heartily at his own indulgence. His pale, soft, heavy hands were covered with a pelt of thick grey hair on the back, and when he was out of church his pudgy fingers were always tamping down the barrel of his briar pipe, or lighting it up with a miniature flame-thrower.

He was a busy, happy, popular priest, always ready with a kind word and a joke and a bit of practical help for the inadequate drifters and no-hopers who frequently crossed his path.

The Presbytery where he lived with his spinster sister as housekeeper was built in the same architectural style as the church, with ogival windows and little Gothic turrets and gargoyles, and a weather-beaten statue of St. Patrick in a niche over the front door. The Presbytery stood a couple of hundred yards away from the church, separated from it by an expanse of lawn and flower-beds and a thriving avenue of lime trees.

The heavy iron-studded oak front door was never locked, as a gesture of the priest's supreme faith in his humble community. In all the years he'd been there nobody had ever intruded into the Presbytery, or stolen so much as a bottle of communion wine.

One evening near the end of May at eleven o'clock the Father was at work in his study, beavering away at the accounts of his numerous fund-raising schemes. Miss Marcella Fogarty-Fegan, his fifty-year-old spinster sister was in the kitchen, washing up the mugs which had contained their late-night cocoa. Neither of them heard the faint creak of the front door as it was opened from outside, and a dark figure slipped inside the quiet Presbytery.

He was dressed in a dirty old boiler suit,

with a woollen hat pulled down over his head and a scarf tied round the lower part of his face. He looked a frightening faceless figure, all the more menacing because he moved with complete silence.

When Miss Marcella turned round from the kitchen sink, he was there right behind her, and she hadn't heard a thing. She caught her breath with terror, and her intended scream was no more than a ghastly croak, as she stood there petrified with the shock of meeting the Devil. Her first coherent reaction was to try to make the sign of the cross to exorcise the monstrous apparition. Before she could move a muscle, the gruesome figure grabbed her by the arms, wheeled her round and rammed a length of cotton wool in her mouth, which he secured there by knotting a length of dirty cloth. Then he tied her hands together with a piece of electric flex, tied up her ankles in the same way, and bundled her into a tall broom cupboard whose door could be unlatched only from outside. Not a word had been spoken.

Swiftly the intruder moved out of the kitchen, down the corridor to the room at the far end where he'd seen there was a light on. Father Fogarty-Fegan glanced up from his accounts as the door opened, expecting his sister who usually came in to say goodnight.

Then he tensed, bolt upright in shock and indignation, as he saw the intimidating figure of the interloper. But he kept his cool and tried to be conciliatory, believing that even the most wicked villain, unhappily afflicted with more than his share of original sin, would respect the saintly gentleness of a priest.

'Yes, my son? Who are you? What do you want from me?'

The intruder spoke in a deep, menacing voice.

'Do you remember Bernadette Faldo who used to come to you to make her confession?'

'Ah, indeed I do, the poor lassie. Buried only yesterday with her man. What a shocking business, to be sure.'

'You hypocritical bastard! You're the one who caused those deaths.'

'Goodness gracious me! What's that you're saying?' gasped the priest in a tone of shocked incredulity.

'I'm saying you betrayed the secret of the confessional.'

'Indeed I did not! In all the years in the

priesthood I've never done such a wicked thing.'

'There's no other answer. I've checked all those confession boxes in the church, and none of them are wired. There's not a bug anywhere near them. So you were the only one who could have passed on the information she gave you. She told nobody else because she was too scared.'

'My son, this is a terrible accusation you are making. No Catholic priest would ever betray the confessional. Indeed it would be a mortal sin.'

'She told you in her confession that her brother-in-law was staying in the house, a discharged S.A.S. man, with a kitbag full of weapons.'

'You're saying that, my son, not me,' countered the priest firmly.

'You passed the knowledge on to some mick bastard here in London who's in touch with the I.R.A. in Belfast.'

'No! 'Tis a wicked lie,' blustered the priest, turning pale.

'They promptly sent a murder squad to London to kill the reported S.A.S. man, but the orders got bungled somewhere along the line, and they killed a harmless clockmaker and his wife, just because he hap-

123

pened to have the same name, Faldo.'

The priest closed his eyes and folded his hands together, and his lips moved in silent prayer, pleading for this monstrous ordeal to be taken away from him.

'Do you hear what I'm saying, you oily old bastard? You killed those two people as surely as if you'd fired the machine gun yourself.'

'Oh, dear God!' gasped the priest. 'I don't believe this is happening to me. 'Tis some terrible nightmare, to be sure. What have I done to deserve it?'

'You know damned well what you've done,' went on his accuser relentlessly. 'Mixed your politics up with your bloody praying, didn't you, and now the bill's come in. You might be a professional liar with an elastic conscience, but you can't do a soft-shoe shuffle out of this. Come along now, Father. I want to know who you passed the news from the confessional on to. Give me a name.'

'What news did I pass on?'

'About Faldo, the S.A.S. man, living in Camberwell at a clockmaker's shop.'

'But you're wrong, my son. You're terribly and wilfully wrong, so you are,' complained the priest desperately. 'Be a good fellow.

Have a drink and be on your way now.'

'I'll be on my way soon enough when you've told me what I want to know. Who did you drop a hint to, about that little gem in Bernadette's confession?'

'I did not betray the confessional. I did not.'

'I can see it's going to be a long, cold night,' said the intruder menacingly.

'And what might that mean?'

'One of your own kind would have shot our kneecaps off by now, but I don't go in for that kind of savagery. I'll take a bit longer over it. But I'm going to get the truth from you before I leave. Why not save yourself a lot of aggravation, Father? And if you've any Christian charity left in your heart, spare a thought for the old girl I met in the kitchen. She'll be grateful if you don't spin it out too long.'

'My sister!' exclaimed the priest, starting up in alarm. 'What have you done to her, you devil?'

'Talk to me, Father. Who's the I.R.A. undercover man you're in touch with? Give me a name, and then I may give you plenary absolution.'

# FOURTEEN

'That's an ugly business over in Camberwell,' said Detective Chief Inspector Sperling as he greeted Detective Sergeant Shindler in his office. 'Some bloody animal's just killed a Catholic priest in his own Presbytery.'

'Doesn't surprise me, guv,' retorted Shindler wearily. 'The old and the sick and the priesthood who used to be sacrosanct are considered a soft touch nowadays. They only exist to be ripped off. Even the teeny-boppers are mugging and torturing old pensioners in their homes, to get their miserable pittance off them. It's the climate of opinion in your civilised state.'

'The doors of the Presbytery were never locked or bolted,' went on Sperling. 'Father Fogarty-Fegan liked to show that he trusted his flock and didn't erect any barriers against the drifters, drop-outs and no-hopers.'

'So he had to be disappointed some time, didn't he? What were they after, the chalice, the candlesticks, or the communion wine?'

'That's what's so strange. Not a damned thing was stolen. Nothing was broken, vandalised or desecrated. The priest's spinster sister who lives there as house-keeper was tied up and gagged and shoved into a broom cupboard. She was shaken but undamaged, and able to state that there was only one assailant, masked and anonymous of course, and he never spoke a word.'

'Some bloody deranged spook trying to haul his sterile ashes, and needing a cassock to turn him on,' exclaimed Shindler with heavy disgust. 'I've heard it all now. But why did he spare the spinster and kill the priest?'

'Preliminary reports indicate that Father Fogarty-Fegan died of a massive cerebral stroke some hours after the assailant left. But he had been knocked about, physically assaulted in a fairly protracted ordeal that probably brought on the stroke. In fact there are certain indications in the punish-ment he took that would suggest he was tortured.'

'Really?' said Shindler, interested in spite of his blasé acceptance of the worst. 'Now I wonder what kind of maniac would want to torture a Catholic priest, unless he's a new-wave religious nut, trying to put the

Inquisition into reverse.'

'They shoot Catholics every day in Ireland, don't they?' mused the chief inspector.

'Ah,' said Shindler, 'now there's a thought. Camberwell is where the Faldos were killed by the I.R.A. I bet they knew that priest. What was his name again?'

'Father Niall Daniel Fogarty-Fegan.'

'A decent, well-bred Irish name, to be sure,' nodded Shindler. 'The Irish dimension again, guv. No escape from it in this city, is there?'

'It was his assistant priest who found him at seven o'clock in the morning,' said Sperling. 'The Father was supposed to be celebrating early Mass in St. Patrick's, and he didn't turn up. As he'd never been known to be late in his life, his side-kick goes over to the Presbytery to see what's happened. He hears this feeble kicking from inside a broom cupboard in the kitchen, and sets free the sister. They find the priest flaked out in his study, close to death. They got a doctor to him but it was too late. Just before he died he croaked out three syllables in delirium. It sounded like S.O.S., and everybody's wondering why.'

'Good God!' exclaimed Shindler. 'I'm not wondering why. He didn't say S.O.S. He said S.A.S., that brings us right up against our current problem. His assailant must have been that crazy bastard Faldo, who's on the rampage because the micks killed his brother instead of him. But I wonder why he had to go and knock over an old Catholic priest. Not much of a challenge for an S.A.S. man. I would have thought there are plenty of other micks in London he could have gone after, if he's only out for Irish blood.'

'Unless he wanted something in particular from the priest,' mused Sperling. 'There's no other feasible explanation for the torture symptoms. Unless he's a complete maniac – and he didn't give me that impression – there's no other reason why he should knock an old priest about and cause him to have a stroke.'

'If you're right, guv, and he got the information he wanted from the priest, we can expect a continuation of murder and mayhem on the streets. The S.A.S. and the I.R.A. playing tit-for-tat like daft kids, but it's no laughing matter.'

'Why hasn't there been any progress in picking Faldo up?' demanded the chief inspector with a frown. 'We know he's here in London, playing God towards his enemies, and yet he comes and goes with impunity.'

'We can't get a fix on him any way at all, guv,' complained Shindler. 'We've checked with the Ministry of Defence and Northern Ireland Army H.Q. in Lisburn, and they can't give us an address where he might be holed up, apart from Harry Faldo's clock shop in Camberwell. He has no other living relatives. His brother was the sole surviving member of his family, and now he's gone we reckon Faldo must be living rough. He's got the know-how to blend in with the background, and there's no shortage of human derelicts to blend with. We've got men dressed as drop-outs hanging about the doss-houses, hostels and soup kitchens. We've got a twenty-four hour watch on the Lambeth and Camberwell spikes, just in case the foul weather drives him in for a bit of shelter. We're bound to get a line on him before long.'

'Have you stressed how dangerous this man can be?'

'Yes, guv. They know the score. It's taken for granted Faldo knows where to put his hand on a shooter when he needs one, and that he's a cold, clinical, precision killer like all his outfit. Nobody's likely to forget what they did to those murdering wogs who took over the Iranian embassy. They killed the bloody lot in two minutes flat, and one of the terrorists had thirty-nine bullets in him. Well, we've got one of those buggers gone mad on us, back from years of practice in Ireland, unrestrained by any corporate discipline, and out to kill as many micks as he can for personal revenge. That's what it looks like to me.'

'Well, keep me informed,' said the chief inspector. 'Let's hope we can box him in somewhere before there are any more fatalities.'

As it happened, they picked up Faldo a couple of days later with no trouble.

Detective Constable Pearson, on the drop-out patrol, chanced to see the shabby, non-descript figure saunter casually into a small café for poor folk in a run-down street in Brockley. The café was of the greasy spoon variety, where you could get stewed tea, a wedge of bread and marge and a greasy fry-up for less than a quid.

Despite his chameleon-like blending into the grey background of no-hope and poverty, Faldo was recognisable to the trained eye because he looked younger, fitter and somehow more purposeful than the other flotsam. Though dressed almost exactly like them, he was worlds apart from the shambling derelicts who were so prematurely aged by despair and deprivation.

Detective Constable Pearson sat down at the rickety table where Faldo was wolfing his chips from a cracked plate on a stained table-cloth.

'Sergeant Faldo, I presume,' he said.

The man looked up at him with an icy glint in his greyish green eyes and carried on eating. The detective introduced himself and showed his warrant card.

'I'd like you to come with me to the Police Station, Mr. Faldo.'

'Why?'

'There are some questions we have to ask you in connection with certain offences that have been committed.'

'What's the charge?' growled Faldo.

'We don't prefer charges until we've established that there's a case to answer. This is just a routine enquiry.'

'Suppose I don't want to come?'

'Let's not make that supposition,' said the detective hastily. 'Why put yourself in the same class as petty thieves, pushers and other creeps if you've nothing to hide?'

Faldo shrugged indifferently.

'Am I allowed to finish my dinner?' he said ironically.

'Of course. There's no hurry,' replied the detective conciliatingly. 'I've got a car in the next street when you're ready.'

'You won't mind if I make a phone call from here to my lawyer?'

Detective Constable Pearson hesitated, unsure of himself.

'Well, we'd prefer you to do it from the Station.'

'What for? There's a phone on the wall over there. Everybody knows the condemned man is allowed the privilege of one phone call.'

'Oh, all right then. Make it from here.'

Having finished his meal in leisurely fashion and made his phone call, Faldo submitted with a kind of stoical docility to be driven to Catford Police Station. A quarter of an hour later he was sitting in the same interview room as he'd been in before, facing Detective Chief Inspector Sperling across the scarred and grimy deal table.

'Where were you on the night of May the thirtieth, last Saturday, to be precise?' said the chief inspector abruptly.

'I couldn't say. Probably in a pub.'

133

'I mean in the small hours when the pubs are shut.'

'Asleep of course, in some hostel or doss-house. I'm of no fixed abode, remember.'

'Which doss-house?'

'The Camberwell spike or the Sally Army or Bennett House. Take your pick. I can't really remember.'

'We've checked all the hostels and reception centres recently, and nobody remembers you being there on Saturday night.'

'Why should they? They deal with hundreds of dossers every night.'

'What about the Roman Catholic Presbytery in Camberwell?' said Sperling suddenly.

'What about it?'

'Did you go there on Saturday night?'

'No. What would I want with a priest house?'

'What indeed! I think it was you who forcibly entered the house and assaulted the priest and his elderly sister.'

Faldo returned his gaze coolly without a flicker.

'The priest died of a stroke some hours later, almost certainly brought on by his injuries. It was a vicious, dastardly attack, and it certainly won't go unpunished.'

'Well, it's all very unfortunate,' shrugged Faldo, 'but I don't see what it's got to do with me.'

'Before he died the priest was heard to mutter S.A.S., which points very strongly to you. We know of no other man recently discharged from the S.A.S., and with a heavy score to settle against the Irish.'

'That's your suspicious mind, Inspector,' retorted Faldo indifferently. 'You know as well as I do it's certainly not evidence.'

'The priest's sister caught sight of the assailant before he locked her in the broom cupboard,' went on Sperling, watching him keenly.

'Oh, good. Then you'd better put me up for identification, and settle it once and for all. Let the old girl pick me out from twelve others if I was really there.'

'We're going to have to take your finger-prints of course,' said the chief inspector, changing tack.

'What for?' said Faldo, very much amused. 'Do you reckon you'll find my dabs all over the priest house?'

'That's something we have to find out, isn't it?'

Detective Sergeant Shindler took Faldo downstairs to the finger-print department, and one by one each of his fingers was rolled on the inky pad and pressed on a sheet of white paper to leave its imprint.

By the time that routine had been gone through, Faldo's solicitor had arrived at the Station, and was loudly demanding access to his client. His name was Joshua Betts of New Cross, and he considered it his vocation to defend the poor and the underprivileged from the rough-shod persecution of pushy policemen out to get easy convictions at the expense of the feckless and ignorant.

Betts was a small, round-shouldered man with a pronounced limp, one leg being several inches shorter than the other after a serious motor cycle accident in his youth. He had a high bald dome adorned with one long wisp of straggling grey hair. His round red cheeks, red button of a nose and owl-like granny glasses made him look like a garden gnome. But there was nothing of the buffoon about him when savaging a police witness in a court of law. His gnome-like head and prominent Adam's apple bobbed up and down in unison as he ranted with righteous eloquence. He enjoyed a glowing reputation among the sub-community for his immediate assumption of a client's innocence, no matter what the evidence stacked against him, and for his fearless, tireless, often unscrupulous efforts to defeat and discredit the common enemy, the police.

Detective Chief Inspector Sperling regarded this legal prestidigitator with the acute distaste that fighting men in an army have for the ghouls who come after the battle to bury the dead, to relieve them of their rings and watches and empty their pockets before slinging them in an old army blanket for burial.

Faldo had gone to Joshua Betts immediately after his first run-in with Shindler and Neilson, complaining bitterly of how he'd been picked up on sus in the cemetery, taken in and grilled merely because of his presence at his brother's funeral. To Betts it was a blatant case of police persecution against Faldo, merely because of his former association with an élite regiment, very much in the public eye for its deadly efficiency. The police had formed a bigoted pre-conception of Faldo's criminal capability, but you couldn't give a dog a bad name and hang him nowadays, as Betts lost no time in pointing out to the chief inspector.

When the questioning of Faldo was

resumed, the lawyer insisted on being present, and went a good way towards putting the police on the defensive.

'Now, Mr. Faldo,' said Sperling, 'how well did you know the deceased Catford book-maker, Ian Melling?'

'I didn't,' replied Faldo flatly.

'I think you did. You knew him as the veteran I.R.A. gunman Kiernan O'Malley, and you came to London immediately after your discharge from the Army to settle old scores.'

'I don't believe I'm hearing this!' scoffed the little gnome-like lawyer. 'It's pushing pure, unsubstantiated conjecture to ludicrous limits. My client doesn't even need to answer such wild accusations.'

'Where were you on the night of May the tenth?' snapped the chief inspector.

'I was staying with my brother in the rooms above his shop in Camberwell. Unfortunately he's not here to verify it, but I never left my room all night or any night while I stayed there.'

'Did you ever borrow your brother's three-wheeled invalid car while you were there?'

'What if I did?' said Faldo looking cagey. 'What's that got to do with anything?'

'I'm asking the questions,' snapped Sperling irritably. 'Answer yes or no.'

'All right, no!'

'In that case, would you care to explain how your finger-prints and palm prints came to be all over the vehicle? They're more numerous there than the rightful owner's.'

'Oh, well,' muttered Faldo, rather badly rattled, 'the old heap was a poor starter when it was cold. Harry was always having trouble starting it, and as he was no good with engines, I helped him out.'

'Our technicians' examination of the vehicle didn't reveal any starting difficulties,' retorted the chief inspector triumphantly. 'The engine was in perfect condition and started every time at the first turn of the starter.'

Faldo was silent, taken aback, and glanced towards his lawyer for support.

'From the position of your hand-prints all over the body work, it looks as if you had to push the car some distance. Why would you want to do that, Mr. Faldo, if the vehicle was mechanically sound and not short of petrol?'

'Excuse me, Chief Inspector,' interposed the lawyer scathingly, 'but these questions are a complete nonsense and waste of time as far as I'm concerned. Of what shattering importance is it that my client tinkered with his brother's invalid car while he was staying there?'

'Just bear with me a minute, Mr. Betts,' said the chief inspector smoothly. 'After certain enquiries we now regard Mr. Faldo as a suspect for the murder of Ian Melling of Lewisham Park Road on the night of May the tenth. We have a witness, a householder in the same road two hundred yards away from Melling's flat, who's testified that a three-wheeled invalid car was parked outside her house at the time of the actual murder. Now with our knowledge of the dead man's past associations, and Mr. Faldo's former military involvement with them, is it being wildly fanciful to see the strong probability that the Faldo invalid car could have been the one at the scene of the crime?'

'Good God!' exclaimed Betts, throwing up his hands in mock horror. 'I hear this and I don't believe it! Certainly not from a chief inspector. Did your householder witness take the registration number of the invalid car parked outside his house?'

'No. She couldn't make out the number from her upstairs window in artificial light.'

'And did she observe the colour of the vehicle?'

'No accurate observation of colour can be made in sodium lighting, as you very well know. All colours show as grey.'

'Then on what grounds other than prejudice do you assume that the invalid car in question was the Faldo car?'

'It's just a strong indication. I didn't say it was hard evidence,' replied the chief inspector, controlling his temper with difficulty.

'Do you know how many of those N.H.S. three-wheeled invalid carriages there are at this moment in the London area?'

'No.'

'No. And I bet you haven't taken the trouble to find out either. Why hasn't the owner of every invalid car been traced and interviewed, together with all his male relatives, if you suspect that the vehicle left in Lewisham Park Road at the material time could have belonged to the killer? I can't help feeling, Chief Inspector, that you have a completely closed mind on the subject of my client's guilt. You're trimming and tailoring the evidence to support your own neat little theory of a crime and its antecedents, just because you believe that my client with his S.A.S. background is a likely customer. Let me remind you that you're perpetrating an evil slander on a fine regiment.'

'He still hasn't given me a satisfactory explanation as to why his handprints are all over the invalid car's bodywork,' retorted Sperling doggedly. 'I suggest that he pushed it out of the yard and well away from his brother's house before starting it up because it has a noisy and distinctive engine note, which might have awakened his brother and wife and made them suspicious. He didn't want them to know he was out that night and in need of transport, for obvious reasons.'

'Well, Mr. Faldo,' said Betts genially, 'I'm sure you have a perfectly feasible alternative explanation for those prints on the car.'

'Of course,' said Faldo smoothly. 'My brother wasn't very expert at manoeuvring the car under its shed. He often stalled it going in and had to be pushed the last couple of feet. As he had difficulty in pushing anything because of his disability, I used to do it for him while I was there.'

'Perfectly reasonable, perfectly acceptable,' applauded the lawyer. 'Are you convinced now, Chief Inspector? I suggest you drop this whole line of enquiry in trying to connect my client with the Melling murder. It's a dead duck, as also is your equally desperate attempt to implicate him in the crime at the Camberwell Presbytery.'

'I'm not convinced of that,' replied Sperling stubbornly. 'With his last breath the dying priest gasped the letters, S.A.S., and we can't trace anybody else in the area except Faldo who has a connection with that regiment.'

'Then you're going to charge him with the attack on the priest?' snapped Betts.

'Not until further enquiries have been completed,' replied the chief inspector cautiously.

'Good. That's one monumental blunder you seem capable of avoiding. So there's no need to detain him further. You'll be setting Mr. Faldo at liberty as of this moment.'

'Well, that's a different proposition altogether,' replied Sperling shortly. 'In view of the strong grounds for suspicion against him and the serious nature of the crimes–'

'Come on now!' exclaimed Betts roughly. 'That simply will not do. You've admitted that you have insufficient evidence to charge my client, so how can you possibly justify holding him in custody a minute longer? It contravenes the whole letter and the spirit of the new Bail Act. Are there any further questions you wish to put to him?'

'Not at present.'

'Very well then. It's incumbent on you to release him now. Otherwise I shall stay here with him while my partner goes before a Judge in chambers to seek an injunction against your unlawful detention of an innocent man.'

The detective and the lawyer glowered at each other without speaking, each one convinced of his own unassailable rectitude in upholding the law.

'I hope you realise the weight of your responsibility in letting this man loose on the streets when there are so many serious questions about him,' said the chief inspector coldly. 'You realise that your pig-headed self-righteousness over this could cost the life of somebody you don't even know?'

'Rubbish! You show me one piece of serious evidence that my client is a dangerous psychopath or a homicidal maniac, and I'll gladly join with you in locking him away,' said Betts equally coldly. 'But you've nothing to support your hypothesis, and that's not good enough to deprive a man of his liberty. You have to charge him or let him go.'

'I'm just paying the price of being an innocent bystander,' complained Faldo bitterly. 'I had my last surviving relatives shot down around me by sub-human micks, and then the bloody sky fell in on me because I went to the funeral. These incompetent cozzers are trying to screw me for every bloody crime in London.'

The chief inspector gave an irritated gesture of dismissal, realising that the rights and privileges of villains were always too well stacked to the disadvantage of law enforcement.

'All right,' he growled. 'You can go, Faldo. I haven't the legal clout to hold you against the machinations of bloody lawyers. But we've got your number now, so you'd better watch it. There's been a high death-rate among the Irish since you came to town, and I don't want any more of it.'

Once again, as soon as Faldo had left the Police Station, a detective set out to shadow him, to find out where he went to ground and monitor all his movements. But within twenty-four hours Faldo had given him the slip and vanished again into that seedy twilight world of homeless vagrants, squats, hostels, soup kitchens and spikes, where a man who loved freedom could live unsupervised by his betters.

# FIFTEEN

Donald O'Dowd of the Liffey Bridge Hotel in Wandsworth was always a fairly light sleeper, even after getting well tanked up. He slept apart from his wife Sile, at her insistence, in a room on the first floor, for they'd given up sex after the fifth child, and his wife could no longer stand his beery snoring or other gross bedroom habits. The arrangement suited Don all right, for in the sanctity of his own room at dead of night he was able to invite room service from his current favourite on the hotel staff.

The recent savage death of his real favourite, Rosyn Fitzgerald, had left him saddened, disturbed and deeply worried. He'd carried a torch for her even though he'd always known that she wasn't really interested in sex like a normal, loving woman. Her first love, indeed her only love was the Irish Republican Cause and the recovery of the six counties by fire and bloodshed. She'd humoured O'Dowd's passionate and sentimental love for her and allowed him his *droit de seigneur* because she was a proud girl who accepted charity from no one. She'd had no other means of repaying him for the board and lodging which she so sorely needed in London after her bitter quarrel over strategy with Kiernan O'Malley.

O'Dowd hadn't known or wanted to know what political activity she was involved in. But he knew now that it was the cause of her hideous death, as also was the case with the revered patriot, Kiernan O'Malley, whose violent demise had preceded hers by only a few days. The old wicked war had followed them across the water. O'Dowd couldn't help being worried sick by the awful fear that the same lightning that had struck them down might also fall on him and his: on Sile and the children. Guilt by association, even though he was no longer politically active.

When an unidentified noise suddenly snapped him out of sleep at two a.m., he sat bolt upright in the bed, breaking out in a cold sweat. He knew it couldn't be one of the girls. They came only by invitation, and they slipped noiselessly through the door, bare-foot and bare-back, in order not to waken Sile next door.

O'Dowd listened intently and it came

again, the clumsy noise of somebody moving about in the bar immediately beneath his bedroom, the furtive clink of a glass, as if somebody was getting himself a drink. O'Dowd climbed quietly out of bed, knowing that he had to do something about it. He couldn't just lie there and wait for the intruder to go away. With a bit of luck it might turn out to be only Fergus the potman, helping himself to a hair of the dog, or one of the girls who'd brought her feller in for a late snifter and a cuddle in the warmth.

He crept down the carpeted stairway, feeling his way in the dark. At the foot of the stairs he groped cautiously round the big square newel post to the umbrella stand, and slowly extracted a heavy-duty walking stick of knotty ash. He walked softly down the passage to the door of the public bar which was just ajar, and peered cautiously round into the pool of darkness where the intruder must be.

Suddenly he saw movement, and a figure was dimly outlined against the faint glow which came through the curtains from the street lighting outside. Judging by the size of the silhouette, it was a man at least six feet tall. O'Dowd gripped his walking stick firmly, determined not to back off no matter how big the intruder was.

He felt round the wall inside the room to where the bar-room switches were, and with one brusque movement suddenly illuminated the whole scene in a full battery of blazing light that temporarily blinded O'Dowd himself. As his eyes adjusted, he took in the scene.

The startled intruder was standing frozen by the bar counter with a glass in his hand. He was a tall, well-built negro boy of about eighteen, with a big mop of candyfloss hair in the Afro style. He had long legs and long dangling arms. He was dressed in threadbare denim jeans, grubby off-white sweat shirt, simulated leather jacket and scuffed canvas sneakers, the street uniform of unemployed blacks.

He put his hand over his eyes to shut out the blinding light, and recoiled unsteadily as if the worse for drink. Judging by the half-empty bottle of O'Dowd's whisky open on the counter, he had reason to be unsteady on his pins.

'And what the hell might you be doing here, you thieving black bastard?' demanded O'Dowd fiercely, raising his knotty ash in a menacing gesture. 'Sure I don't know whether to break your black skull before I hand you over to the police.'

'No, please, no, Mr. O'Dowd,' pleaded the negro abjectly. 'Please don't grass me to the Man. They always movin' me on, havin' me in on sus, pushin' me around and callin' me Jim Crow. They catch me on this, man, and they bust my ass for sure.'

'And not before time, so it is, you thievin' scum,' snarled the hotelier. 'Knockin' back my liquor at five quid a bottle, they should throw away the key!'

He moved behind the bar and picked up the handset of the telephone under the counter.

'Oh, please, man, Mr. O'Dowd,' whined the negro. 'You don' unnerstand. She said you a good man. She said to come to you if I was ever in any trouble.'

O'Dowd stopped abruptly with his finger in the telephone dial.

'She!' he exclaimed sharply. 'What she? Who the hell are you talking about?'

'Miz Fitzgerald, man. Rosyn Fitzgerald. She my friend, till some spook stick her with a chiv.'

'Holy Jesus!' exclaimed O'Dowd incredulously, slamming the receiver back on its cradle. 'I don't believe it.'

'It the gospel truth, man. She tell me how

you let her live here when she got nowhere else to go, because you a good man.'

The hotelier was impressed despite his hostility and suspicion.

'Look, Sambo, who are you? What's your name?'

'I Leroy Green, and I don't have no mammy nor no pappy. I live with my Aunt Ada and her eight chillen in Brockley, Beechcroft Road. Leastways I did, till the Panthers came after me.'

'The Panthers? Talk some sense, Leroy Green. Who the hell are the Panthers?'

'They a street gang, man, in Brockley. Larry Tumber is the boss, a real hard dude. They mug whitey, steal his cars, break in his shops, take over his women for gang-bangs. I a member of the Panthers till Larry Tumber started gettin' too big and hard. He's out for the Big Time. He wants to take this warehouse, man, all full of colour T.V. sets and Hi-fi. He wants me to steal a furniture van to take the gear away in. But man, that too heavy for me, so I chicken out of that action.'

'Stop bullshitting, Green, and get to the point,' interrupted O'Dowd impatiently. 'What's all this got to do with Rosyn Fitzgerald?'

'I gettin' there, man. Don't race your motor. This Larry Tumber, he has to steal his own furniture van for the heist. But when he backed it in the warehouse yard and they started loading up, suddenly the lights go on, everybody starts shoutin', and the whole scene alive with fuzz. Yeah, man, the Panthers all got nicked by the Man. So then they say it that chicken shit Uncle Tom coon Leroy Green who grassed. He chickened out because he already finked to the Man. It wasn't me who grassed. No way. But the Panthers they fingered me all the same. They all out on bail, and they come after me. They throw bricks through Aunt Ada's front window. They tie a dead cat to her door. They paint *Death to the Green Fink* in green paint all over her front wall. Man, I had to leave home fast for Aunt Ada and all her chillen's sake.

'I come over here to Wandsworth lookin' for a squat, but the Panthers they been followin' me around, and they there, too, man. They chase me down Wandsworth High Street into York Road. They right behind me with their chivs and bike chains, and I all bushed, man, bushed, all set to go through the bacon slicer.

'Then I see this taxi coming down the

road behind me with the lovely white lady in the back seat. She see me runnin' fit to drop, and all the Panther's comin' up fast behind, yelling and waving their chivs. She tell the driver to slow down alongside o' me, and then she open the back door.

'Get in, man. Quick!' she say. And I didn't need askin' twice.

'I got in, she slammed the door, and tole the driver to move it. I hear them Panthers yelling with rage right behind, but I'm away, man, free and clear. And that's how I got to know Rosyn Fitzgerald. I reckon I owes her my life.

'She ask me what I was into, and I tole her all about the Panthers. She ask me what I was a-goin' to do, and I say I lookin' for a squat, an empty, wrecked old house with nobody else in it, so I could live in peace and just do my own thing. Then she say she needed that sort of a place as well to store some gear that she didn't want nobody else to know about. As I owed her one, she say, I could let her know when I scored and look after this gear for her.

'So that's what I did, man. I found this old house in Wandsworth near the river in Kersey Road. Been empty for years. All the windows and doors got corrugated iron sheets nailed over 'em to keep out squatters like me. But I have a look round the back and get a crow bar to lever one sheet away at the corner so I could squeeze inside. Soon as I got settled in, I come here and ask to see Rosyn so I could take her and show her the place.

'She move in her gear, a bagful at a time, hide it in the cellar behind some old junk furniture.'

'You're putting me on!' exclaimed O'Dowd incredulously. 'What sort of gear would Rosyn have that she couldn't keep in her room here? Why should she want to keep it in a wrecked old house?'

'This kind of stuff,' said Leroy Green, suddenly pulling a 36 grenade from the pocket of his leather jacket, and standing it upright on the counter. It stood on its base-plug like an evil little pineapple, a standard infantry weapon of the British Army in two world wars. Three red crosses painted on its fragmentation squares showed that it had been to the ordnance factory to be filled with high explosive.

O'Dowd stared at it in disbelief and recoiled instinctively.

'Holy Mary!' he muttered. 'She was a close one, to be sure. I had no idea that she was still working in the front line. How many of 'em did you say she'd got?'

'About a dozen,' said Leroy Green, 'and there's guns as well, automatic pistols and magnums and Sterling sub-machine guns stripped down. Rosyn say she storing them for a new Active Service Unit comin' over from Dublin in case the Brits don't grant the demands of the hunger strikers in the H-Blocks. Very hush-hush.'

'And she never told me a thing, to be sure, not a whisper!' muttered O'Dowd sadly. 'It's almost as if she didn't trust me.'

'She say she didn't want you to land in no trouble because you got a family to think of. If the Man find any of that stuff here you'd be deported for sure, and lose your hotel. She wasn't going to risk that because you'd done a lot for her.'

'God bless her!' whispered O'Dowd, with large tears forming in his eyes. 'That was Rosyn all over, a sweet, kind, generous little girl. She was always thinking of others, never of herself.'

'She tell me you a good man, on her side, a man to be trusted,' went on Leroy Green earnestly. 'She tell me iffen I ever in trouble I come here and mention her name, and you know what to do.'

'And what sort of trouble are you in then?' growled O'Dowd. 'The Panthers again or the police?'

'Not me, man. I ain't in no real trouble now. I could just blow the scene and forget it. But yesterday there's a bunch of hippies moved in on me in my squat in Kersey Road. They taken over all the rooms, and as they six to one, not countin' their women and chillen, I ain't about to give 'em no argument, no way, man.

'They went down in the cellar and started bustin' up this junk furniture to light fires. Any time at all now, man, they's goin' to get to the back and find these four zippered-up bags with the guns and bombs and ammunition. So I thought, as Rosyn my friend and I still owed her one, I come here at night and tip you off about this gear she got stashed away in my squat. Yeah man, she'd have wanted me to do that after she was dead. You'd know what to do with 'em better than a lousy bunch of hippies. You on Rosyn's side and maybe do what she wanted. So that's all I came to say, Mr. O'Dowd, and iffen it's all the same to you I guess I'll be on my way. Unless you still goin' to hand me over to the Man.'

'No, of course I am not that!' exclaimed

156

O'Dowd hastily. 'I'm beholden to you, Leroy, so I am, even though you gave me one hell of a fright bustin' into my place like this.'

'I didn't bust in, Mr. O'Dowd. I found a kitchen window with a loose catch and got in easy. I figured nobody else had better see me come here, considering I know all about Rosyn's gear.'

'You did absolutely right, Leroy,' said the hotelier approvingly. 'Now where did you say this squat of yours is, just supposing I'm inclined to go there and shift Rosyn's gear to somewhere safer?'

'It's on the corner of Kersey Road, and end of terrace,' said Green. 'Ain't got no number because there ain't no front door, just this sheet of corrugated iron. It facin' Jews Row, only a coupla hundred yards from the big gas depot on the river. Man, you could smell your way there.'

'We could go there right now,' said O'Dowd eagerly. 'I'll get the motor, and you can show me the way.'

'No way, man,' said Leroy firmly. 'You kin go if you want, and risk the aggro from them mean-lookin' hippies. Me, I ain't goin' back there no more. It all gone sour on me, man. I movin' up to Battersea where I knows this dude. You best go in there mob-handed, Mr. O'Dowd. Then you get no trouble from the new owners. Ciao.'

He took another swig from the whisky bottle, waved a limp wrist at the hotelier, and made his way out towards the domestic quarters of the hotel and the kitchen window through which he'd entered. He left the hand grenade still standing menacingly on the bar counter.

O'Dowd picked it up thoughtfully and hefted it. Then with knowledgeable fingers he unscrewed the base plug and swore under his breath when he saw it was primed. He carefully lifted out the U-shaped primer unit of percussion cap, seven-second fuse and detonator, and wrapped it in his handkerchief. He'd always known Rosyn was a damned good soldier, but leaving these babies lying about with the detonators in was a bit on the reckless side, even when working in a two- or three-man cell.

# SIXTEEN

The following night just after midnight an anonymous Ford Cortina drew up in Kersey Road a few yards from the decaying three-storey terrace house that Leroy Green had described as his squat. The melancholy glow of a solitary street light showed a surrounding wasteland, a row of grey boarded-up houses with the yards at the back weedy and forlorn, strewn with the detritus of years of sub-standard living. Dead factories and junk yards crowded in from the middle distance.

Four big men emerged quietly from the car, dressed anonymously in denim jeans and donkey jackets. They carried pick-axe helves as persuaders in case they bumped into trouble, and the leader, Brendan Lamb, carried a Colt magnum as extra insurance. They were a team of hard men from Kilburn who, between them, had notched up a good score of years in English prisons for commonplace crimes of theft and violence. Politically they were republican sympathisers who were always ready to stand up and be counted when there was man's work to be done.

They were all big-bellied fleshy men with the puce faces of hard drinkers, and a burning contempt for the society in which they lived. This lawless mission was right up their street. Brendan Lamb, Raymond Price, Frank Macomber and Eddie Kerrigan had been hand-picked for the job of recovering Rosyn Fitzgerald's secret arms cache, so that it could be put to productive use during the coming summer of violence over the H-Block hunger strikers.

The neglected pavement outside the house was uneven with broken, crumbling slabs and holes washed out by the rain. There was a weed-strewn cinder path round the house with broken terracotta edging tiles to mark the border to what had once been flower-beds. The visitors followed it round to the yard at the back of the house, and found the downstairs window aperture with the corrugated iron sheet hanging loosely from a couple of nails at the top.

Brendan Lamb lifted it up and outwards, enabling the others to duck underneath it and clamber over the sill into the dark interior of the house. Then the others pushed it outward from inside while their leader climbed in. They were immediately assailed by the stench of rotting wood and damp plaster. As they flashed torches round the wrecked interior they saw that some floorboards had been ripped up indiscriminately, so that you had to tread with care in order not to fall through into the cellar. There was dirt and decay everywhere: a pile of plaster in one corner where a ceiling had collapsed; empty bottles and cans and food wrappings thrown down by casual dossers; in an open fireplace the piled-up ashes of countless domestic fires, fuelled by wood from the house fittings and broken-up furniture.

There was an old stained flock mattress with a cheap nylon sleeping bag on it up a corner by the fireplace, but no sign of any occupants. The reported hippies must all be sleeping upstairs, probably stoned out of their minds on speed, grass, or whatever other addiction was in vogue. Nothing could have suited the recovery team better.

'Jesus! What a tip!' muttered Brendan Lamb in disgust. 'What kind of a dumb bastard would ever want to live here? More comfortable in stir, so it is.'

'Kathleen Donoghue trusted him with her

gear, and she knew when a man was man,' whispered Frank Macomber with a lecherous chuckle. 'The coon couldn't have been all that dumb.'

'Where's the bloody cellar then?'

'Under your feet, is it not?'

'I mean the way down to it, for Christ's sake!'

'Hang about a bit,' said Raymond Price. 'It'll be in the front hall sure enough.'

As he started forward his foot kicked a beer can that went skidding raucously over the littered floor.

'Don't make so much bloody noise, you cretin,' hissed the leader angrily. 'We've come to get this gear out all peaceable, with nobody knowing it's ever been here. We do *not* need a bloody ding-dong set-to with half a dozen hippies.'

'There now. That's the front hall-way,' said Raymond Price.

They soon found the door down to the cellar. It was under the staircase, an ordinary cheap panelled door secured by an equally cheap bolt.

'Like a garden shit-house door, so it is,' said Eddie Kerrigan disparagingly.

'Everything just like the coon said,' chuckled Brendan Lamb.

With his comrades clustered around him, he quietly withdrew the bolt from its socket and pushed the cellar door inwards.

Immediately, their world disintegrated in an annihilating sheet of flame, and a great roaring cataclysm engulfed them. The four hard men from Kilburn died without realising that they'd been had by the classic old-fashioned house booby trap. The massive explosion ripped through the crumbling upper floors of the decaying house and erupted through the roof. Sheets of corrugated iron flew out of all the window apertures like corks out of over-pressurised bottles. The force of the blast penetrated the thin dividing wall into the adjoining house, for the two staircases had been positioned side by side to save on building costs.

There was a paraffin heater in use in the house next door, for the occupants came from warmer climes and had to neutralise the perishing cold of a traditional English summer. The nearby explosion shattered the oil tank of the heater and hurled the blazing liquid through the ground floor. Within seconds the house was a blazing inferno, and screams of terror rang out from the upper floors whose windows were veiled with old bedspreads and dirty blankets. For this house was packed from ground floor to roof with Asian squatters. Nobody knew – or if they knew they turned a blind eye to it in the interests of good community relations – that illegal immigrants from the third world, homeless families, as well as coloured criminals on the run, were being found expensive sub-standard accommodation, sleeping in shifts in the condemned house, by a Pakistani *entrepreneur* masquerading as the *bona fide* landlord.

As the hungry flames took hold and spread upward, several of the younger and more active people on the first floor managed to rush down the blazing staircase and out through the front door into the street with their hair singed and their clothes smouldering. Others were swept aside, knocked down and trampled underfoot in the dreadful panic.

But up on the second floor they never stood a chance. Fighting like wild animals to descend the narrow stairway, they were rapidly asphyxiated by the rising smoke, and the only way down was soon completely choked with bodies. Frenzied with fear, mothers started to throw their babies through the windows, and then jumped after them. Asian women in billowing night attire came ballooning down like malfunctioning parachutes. They crashed on the unrelenting pavement to death or serious injury.

Meanwhile there was a Red Alert on at the Wandsworth Gas Depot less than a quarter of a mile away, with bells clanging and sirens wailing. It was naturally assumed at first that this was a gas explosion within the confines of the depot. Minutes after the big bang in the booby-trapped house, fire engines arrived at the scene of the conflagration, and the full extent of the human tragedy was realised.

## SEVENTEEN

It wasn't often that Detective Chief Inspector Sperling called all his men together for a briefing and pep-talk, but he felt obliged to do so in the aftermath of the Wandsworth explosion. Sixteen people had been killed there and as many more seriously injured by falls, burns and smoke inhalation. As forensic experts sifted frantically through the rubble of the two gutted houses for some clue as to the cause of the blast, militant Black Community leaders were loudly spreading the allegation that the disaster was the result of a racial attack on coloured people by white racists, and was therefore mass murder.

As the days went by without any arrest of the authors of the conflagration, black militants accused the police of deliberately dragging their feet in their efforts to find the culprits. Some of the wilder extremists went further, eager to exploit the disaster for political ends, and talked of a police cover-up.

'If half as many white people had been killed by a terrorist attack, the murderers would be in gaol by now.'

Tension mounted in the South London ghettos. Protest demonstrations by thousands of blacks were organised, and in the ensuing confrontations with the police trying to maintain some semblance of civil order on the streets, the waves of violence surged up as far as the seat of government.

'The situation is getting more menacing by the hour,' said the chief inspector grimly. 'It was something far more trivial than this that caused the blacks to run amok in

Brixton and burn the bloody place down. In spite of what the idealists are always telling us about our harmonious multi-racial society, in manors like ours with a high density of coloured population, the under-growth is always tinder-dry, just waiting for a spark like this to set it off. We know who most of the more dangerous left-wing agitators are, so let's keep them under discreet but thorough observation. If there's anybody inciting coloured mobs to rioting, looting and vandalism, we want to know in advance of the insurrection so that we can be ready to contain it.'

'Isn't it time to ban these protest marches altogether?' suggested a middle-aged detective. 'In my time riotous assembly was always considered a criminal offence.'

'That's a political decision for the Home Secretary to take,' said Sperling hastily. 'It's not up to us to try sitting on the safety valve, especially as we're in bad enough odour already with the coloured community.'

'The South Africans must be laughing their bloody heads off at us,' countered the middle-aged one resentfully.

'Have they got anywhere yet in finding what did cause the explosion in the corner house?' enquired Shindler.

'Well, the favourite theory to date is that the house was being used as a bomb factory by a terrorist cell of three or four men, and they got their sums slightly wrong while assembling the devices.'

'Not the bloody Irish, for Christ's sake!' muttered somebody plaintively.

'Forensic evidence points to a powerful form of high explosive in the cellar of the corner house. The gas supply to that street was disconnected years ago at the time of the changeover to North Sea gas. Also, under the rubble of the house they found the remains of three or four men, one of whom was carrying a loaded revolver, a Colt Magnum. One body was sufficiently under-destroyed to give viable finger-prints, and they were on file at the Yard. They belonged to Edward Kerrigan of Kilburn, convictions for theft and making an affray, a known Irish republican sympathiser, who was kept under surveillance by the Anti-Terrorist Squad during the last I.R.A. bombing campaign. But he wasn't seen to be implicated in that – a small-fry hooligan – so they lost interest in him.'

'What about the others, guv? Are they reckoned to be micks as well?'

'It's believed so. Identity of the remains

was impossible to establish. But two of Kerrigan's known associates in Kilburn, Raymond Price and Frank Macomber, fellow villains with similar sympathies and records, disappeared from home at about the same time as Kerrigan and haven't been seen since. The car these people came in was parked in the street and severely damaged by the explosion. It was stolen in Kilburn and had the prints of Kerrigan and Price on the door-handles, and some unknown prints on the steering wheel. So it's pretty conclusive who three of them were.'

'Seems a bit odd, doesn't it?' said Shindler thoughtfully. 'Small time Irish hoods from Kilburn, with no known form or expertise in bomb-making, suddenly coming south of the river to a derelict house in Wandsworth to assemble explosive devices. What was their target? Why were they so far from home? It doesn't smell right to me, guv.'

'I know,' sighed the chief inspector. 'But so far it's the only theory that can possibly fit most of the facts. Irish villains and bomb assembly are a credible enough combination, so their whereabouts at the time of death must surely be of secondary importance. Anyway the Anti-Terrorist Squad are busy rowsting all their contacts and all other republican sympathisers in Kilburn. They're convinced the answer lies there.'

'Well, I'm not,' declared Shindler flatly. 'What about the possibility that the black community leaders have got it right, and it really was a racist scheme to blow up that rabbit warren of poor people next door, but the bomb went off too soon and those micks scored an own goal.'

'That notion doesn't tally with the three dead Irishmen,' objected Sperling. 'I.R.A. men have never been noted for their murderous hostility to coloured people. There's never been a colour problem in Ireland, because New Commonwealth immigrants are sufficiently switched on not to want to go there.'

'But Kerrigan, Macomber and Price could have been bribed by the National Front to set off a bomb next door to that loaded ghetto,' maintained Shindler stubbornly. 'You know how it is with villains, guv. Anything for money. It crosses all barriers of class and creed. It puts more business our way than anything else.'

'Yes, well, let's keep an open mind and not go off into flights of fancy,' replied the chief inspector. 'The fact is that those immigrant families should never have been in the house next door. It's been condemned for years as unfit for human habitation and was awaiting demolition. But a Pakistani empire builder called Mustafa Hafez posed as the landlord to these desperate people, homeless and illegal immigrants, at five quid a week per family, provided they were willing to share a room. I suppose you could say he spotted a gap in the market and went all out to fill it, in the best entrepreneurial tradition.'

'So he's really the bugger who should be hung, drawn and quartered for this disaster!'

'He's passed out of our orbit,' said Sperling resignedly. 'The race relations industry took him under their wing as soon as they heard that the Anti-Terrorist Squad were giving Mustafa some heavy interrogation, trying to tie him in with the Irish connection.'

'An Irish-Pakistani connection, eh?' grumbled Shindler. 'That must be a recipe for the biggest cock-up of all time.'

# EIGHTEEN

Some days later at eleven o'clock one Saturday evening, the Highland Road Police Station was coming under the usual pressure from a feckless, troubled and ungrateful public. The front office was full of complainants, victims and inadequates, each of whom was convinced that the police force functioned for his benefit alone. Even Sergeant Burns, the wally in charge of public relations, who was trying to coast imperturbably along to his pension without acquiring an ulcer or a heart condition, was brow-beaten and harassed almost out of his wits.

An old woman going home from the pub had been mugged by a mob of black youths, and had lost her handbag containing all her money, her pension book and house keys.

A distraught father had arranged to meet his teenage daughter outside a disco, but was informed by her friends that she'd already gone off with some unknown man in a car.

There were three well-dressed, middle-aged burghers, smelling of whisky and expensive cigars, who'd had their company cars pinched from various pub car parks, and were loudly demanding that as they were rate-payers, the police should drop everything else in order to recover the missing vehicles.

A well-dressed Indian professional man, with tears streaming down his cheeks, was confessing that he'd just strangled his eldest daughter after he found her dishonouring him with a man who was not suitable.

A massive, big-bellied docker from the nearby Council flats had dragged in a couple of spiky-haired, ear-ringed and safety-pinned punks by the scruff of their necks, and was loudly proclaiming that he'd just caught them red-handed, shitting in the lift.

'It's a bloody diabolical liberty,' he yelled. 'The place ain't fit for a rat to live in.'

In addition to all this, as if for a bit of light relief, there were the usual drunks reeling about in the office, cursing, weeping, puking, throwing punches and being objectionable in their usual versatile ways.

There seemed no end to it and no way through the shouting, wailing pandemonium surging round the front desk as if to engulf it.

Eventually however, long after midnight, every case had been heard and every grievance taken note of, if not satisfactorily dealt with. The nick seemed to be settling down more peacefully for the rest of the night as Detective Sergeant Shindler came downstairs from his office after putting in an eighteen-hour day.

As he came into the front office the last drunk-and-disorderly was being ushered through to the cells. Sergeant Burns was speaking on the telephone at one end of the counter, and his young assistant, P.C. Randall, had just finished writing in the Incidents Book. He suddenly noticed an electric cycle lamp that one of the night's customers had left on the counter and forgotten. It was just an ordinary lamp on sale in any cycle shop, with a square black body, and the bulb, glass and reflector surrounded by a chromium-plated ring. The on/off switch was a metal knob on top which you pressed and turned.

P.C. Randall idly stretched out his hand to pick it up, his thumb straying automatically towards the on/off switch to test whether it still worked.

At the same moment Detective Sergeant Shindler caught sight of it, and instantly something clicked in his brain with a devastating fear he'd never known before. He knew with a terrible clairvoyance that he was face to face with death. He gave a great roar that made Sergeant Burns drop the telephone, and even startled the stupefied drunks down in the cells.

'DON'T TOUCH IT!' yelled Shindler.

P.C. Randall snatched his hand away as if he'd been scalded, and recoiled a couple of steps back, his face as white as a sheet.

'What the hell's got into you then?' exclaimed Sergeant Burns irritably. 'Jesus wept, man! You'll give me a bloody heart attack.'

'You'd soon be past heart attacks if he touched that switch,' declared Shindler. 'It's a booby trap, a bomb.'

'What!' said Burns incredulously. 'Come off it. You're letting the job get you down. It looks like any other bike lamp to me. Why do you reckon it's a bomb?'

'Because nobody's just going to make us a present of a bike lamp,' snapped Shindler. 'If one of the clients had brought it in with him so it wouldn't get nicked off his bike, he would have remembered as soon as he got outside and needed it. He'd have been back for it long before now, wouldn't he? Has it never crossed your mind that there are spooks and goons and perverts out there who don't like us much? The copper is Aunt Sally to every sick creep nowadays, and especially to buggers with enough know-how to put a bomb together.'

'But it's not ticking,' complained the desk sergeant, bending his ear towards it.

'Of course it's not ticking. It doesn't need a timing mechanism to set it off. Just some silly bugger to turn that switch and complete a circuit is all it needs.'

'What do you recommend we do with it then?' said the desk sergeant in a subdued tone, staring with fascinated horror at the lamp.

'Well, there's not much point in drawing a chalk circle round it,' retorted Shindler tartly.

'There's not a senior officer in the Station. Shall I ring up the Old Man? He'll have my guts if it's a false alarm.'

'He'll have to know about it eventually, so you might just as well wake him up now,' said Shindler. 'Ring up the bomb disposal people as well. This is definitely one for them.'

Turning to the shaking P.C. Randall he said: 'Nip up to my office, son. In the desk, second drawer down on the right, there's an attaché case with a finger-print kit in it. Fetch it down here.'

As P.C. Randall scuttled off upstairs, Sergeant Burns turned a shade paler.

'Here, what the hell are you up to?' he croaked. 'You're not going to mess about with that bloody thing, testing it for dabs?'

'Why not?' retorted Shindler. 'It'll be safe enough as long as I don't touch the switch. That has to be the trigger. The bomb disposal people won't use any finesse in testing it for dabs. They'll just take it away and blow it up and destroy every chance we'll ever have of getting a make on the bastard who delivered it.'

'Yes, well, excuse me,' said Burns, looking green round the gills and backing away hastily. 'I've got to go places. Taken short, you know.'

'I know,' said Shindler with a mirthless grin.

The young wally came back from upstairs with the finger-print kit which he handed to Shindler. Then, his eyes popping with fright, he, too, begged to be excused. He had an urgent call to make and disappeared at a fast trot.

Absolutely alone in the front office

without a sound apart from the distant background murmur of London's night traffic and the occasional nightmare yell from downstairs of a drunk in the cells having a bad trip, Shindler looked at the commonplace bicycle lamp that had his life riding on it, and thought he must be mad.

Cold sweat broke out all over him and the hairs bristled on the back of his neck as he lightly dusted graphite powder over the black metal bodywork of the suspect lamp. As he looked at it through the magnifying glass he saw the pattern of whorls and circular patterns comprising one or two finger and thumb prints, as well as one good section of the heel of a hand.

Carefully pressing strips of Sellotape on to the prints, he peeled them off and stuck them down again on a sheet of white paper, thus effecting an accurate transfer of the finger-print specimens. They were as good as any he'd ever seen taken from the scene of a crime.

With a great feeling of relief and elation, Shindler packed up his finger-print kit and went to tell the two wallies it was safe for them to come out of their bunker and man the desk again. He assured them that the suspected bomb was safe enough as long as nobody touched the switch.

During the course of the night the bomb disposal officer arrived. He was a tall, nonchalant, taciturn man, casually dressed in beret and combat jacket, with a black patch over one empty eye-socket, a face discoloured and disfigured by old skin grafts, and a couple of fingers missing from each hand. He looked at the cycle lamp, smelled it, listened to it and then placed it delicately in a metal container full of cotton wool.

'Have to take it for X-ray,' he said briefly. 'It's definitely a booby trap. I can smell the plastic. Bloody lucky for you you didn't touch that switch. We'll be in touch.'

The subsequent report from the Bomb Disposal Squad on the lethal cycle lamp stated that it contained half a pound of plastic explosive – enough to have wrecked the front office and killed everybody in it at the time – together with a sophisticated electrical detonator powered by four 1.5 volt cadmium cells of the type used in digital watches. The device was considered too dangerous to be dismantled, so it was taken to an army bomb range and blown up.

Detective Sergeant Shindler received high praise and congratulations all round for his perspicacity and quick thinking, which had undoubtedly saved the lives of his two colleagues as well as his own. But what pleased him more than anything else was the report on the finger and hand prints which he'd lifted at such terrible risk from the body of the lamp. When these prints were fed into the Scotland Yard computer, it came up with the name of Leroy Green, an eighteen-year-old West Indian, born and bred in Brockley, with a record of assorted street crime dating from the age of ten: shop-lifting, handbag snatching, picking pockets, driving away cars and motor cycles without the owner's consent, being in possession of drugs, indecent assault on women and girls.

'Well, his record clearly shows he's anti-police, anti-authority and anti-white,' said Chief Inspector Sperling. 'But he didn't dream up this idea of planting a bomb in our nick to cause indiscriminate slaughter, and he certainly didn't construct the booby-trap. He wouldn't know where to get hold of plastic explosive and a suitable detonator. Even less would he know how to wire it up to go off. Some clever bugger put him up to it, bribed or intimidated him into coming in here when the place was a seething mass of complaints, and he wouldn't be noticed. It must be somebody with a real grudge against the police or us in particular. Leroy Green is a Brockley man. We've never felt his collar or even met him on our patch. He has no personal cause to wage a grudge fight against this nick.'

'We'll get the answers when we pick him up, guv,' said Shindler malevolently. 'There's some bastard out there who hates us so much, it's coming out of his ears. And as far as I'm concerned, it's mutual.'

## NINETEEN

The negro was on the run now as he'd never been in his whole life before. He was into something so heavy this time that his friendly probation officer and even the Race Relations Board could never pull him clear. All the other bad things in life, the terrible housing, the impossibility of ever getting a good job, the crude violence of the ghetto, the constant harassment by the police who could always get him on sus as soon as he stepped into the street, all this load was as nothing compared with the trouble he'd been conned into by the white guy who called himself Jim, just for a lousy hundred quid. He still felt bad enough over the trick he'd played on O'Dowd at the Liffey Bridge Hotel, sending him to that booby-trapped house that had caused the death of all those poor people. Didn't that mother know, when he wired up the house, that the pad next door was full of people, or didn't he care?

Even worse for Leroy personally was the trouble he was in for delivering that bike-lamp bomb to the Highland Road nick, leaving it on the counter for some nosey fuzz man to get his ears pinned back with.

Leroy had waited anxiously to read the horrified front-page news of it in all the newspapers, of that lamp exploding and killing a good few fuzz men on their own heap. But nothing had been reported. There was no calamitous tale of fire and destruction at the Highland Road nick, and from a distance it looked exactly the same as usual, with fuzz men and their victims going in and out. Which could only mean that the bomb had failed to go off. Smart-ass Jim had goofed, and that in turn must mean the fuzz had spotted it as a booby-trap and had it made harmless. And now they had possession of it, taking it apart, examining it under a microscope.

Sick with terror Leroy realised that the bomb intact carried its own indictment against him. It had his hand prints all over it, and the Man knew his prints well enough from way back. The fact that they were being so cagey about it at Highland Road and hadn't released a word about it to the newspapers meant that they were up to something.

Leroy Green was going to be the fall guy for that conniving white bastard, Jim, who'd pretended to be his friend. He had to get out of London and fast, even though he had nowhere to go. He hurried on down the road leading south out of London, blinded by headlights, bespattered by the mud from white men's wheels, buffeted by the blast of air from fast moving vehicles only a yard away.

He was wet, tired and hungry. He had money in his pocket, and would have liked to get off the road into the warmth and comfort of a wayside hotel. But he knew the white folks would be suspicious of him, a coloured boy, dressed like he was, with money for hotel bills, most probably stolen. A quick phone call to the Man was all it would take, and that would be the natural recourse for any white hotelier with his built-in hatred of blacks and his wanting to score without getting done by the Race Relations Board.

The further he got from the streets where he grew up, the more lost and despairing he felt, as if he was being pushed away from the breast at feeding time. The only man who'd give him a lift was the driver of a milk float on the outskirts of Sutton on his early morning round: one of Leroy's own kind from Jamaica, grizzled and bowed beneath his load, with a housing problem, a white boss problem, a family problem and an outsize money problem. By the time he'd aired all his grievances to Leroy on the five-mile ride to his depot, Leroy was more depressed than at his own predicament. He was glad to leave the Jamaican milk rounds-man and trudge ahead alone on his own sore feet.

As he plodded southward out of Sutton down a leafy road lined with expensive houses, he suddenly saw a white and blue police patrol car coming towards him with two uniform flat caps in the front seats. Leroy had been conditioned to run at the sight of a police uniform ever since he'd been arrested for his first felony at the age of ten. He knew that they'd automatically pick him up on sus in this ultra-white district even if he acted like a normal law-abiding citizen. The real crime lay in being black.

So he reacted violently with a wild instinctive panic, altered course and started to run up a quiet secluded avenue off the main road. The policemen spotted him and just as instinctively gave chase. The sight of a young West Indian they'd never seen before, with Afro hair style, dressed in leather jacket, jeans and canvas shoes, the uniform of black trouble-makers in the city, was more than sufficient reason for their interest.

The police car roared off down the avenue in pursuit, and as Leroy was already sore-footed and all-in from his long hike, they soon cornered him in the garden of a large house. He put his hands up, palms outward, in a gesture of surrender. They hauled him, panting and exhausted, to his feet and marched him back to their car, where they bundled him into the back seat.

'All right then, chocolate drop, what have you been up to? Why did you run off when you saw us?'

'I ain't done nothin'.'

'What's your name?'

'Charlie Brown,' he replied promptly, reaching for the first alias that came to mind.

'What are you doing here then? You don't live round here.'

'No, sir.'

'You're from the Smoke then?'

'I guess so.'

'Been living rough by the look of it. On the run, are you?'

'No, I sure ain't!' replied Leroy vehemently.

'Well, you'd better come to the Station while we make a few enquiries then. Had any breakfast?'

'No, man.'

'Well, you can have that as a consolation prize. It's on the house, Charlie Brown.'

They took him back to the Sutton Police Station, and put him in an interview room with a standard inmates' breakfast of porridge, bacon and fried bread and tea, while a phone call was made to the Information Room at Scotland Yard about a young negro on the run. On giving the suspect's description they were told they'd probably caught a petty law-breaker called Leroy Green from Brockley, wanted for questioning on the planting of an explosive device in a Catford Police Station.

Formal evidence of identification was obtained by taking his finger-prints and comparing them with Leroy Green's on file at the Yard. An hour later a car arrived to take Leroy Green back to the Highland Road Police Station where he'd planted his incriminating bomb, and where the C.I.D. men were very pleased to see him.

'Now then, Green,' began Detective Chief Inspector Sperling at his most formidable and intimidating, as he opened Green's C.R.O. file. 'I notice you've got a lot of previous convictions, considering your age. You have the makings of a right bloody villain, in fact. But you've never put a foot wrong on our manor, or come to our notice before. So what have you got against us?'

'Nothin' man,' muttered Leroy despairingly.

'Will you kindly tell me then, in words of one syllable that I can understand, why you tried to blow up my police station and cause a blood bath in here?'

'I didn't,' protested Leroy. 'It wasn't me.'

'You expect me to believe that when your prints were found all over the cycle lamp?'

'I mean that lamp wasn't mine. It was

changed for the one on my bike,' said Leroy desperately. 'Some dude must have swung it on me.'

'Rubbish! If you hadn't known exactly what it was, you'd have blown yourself to pieces as soon as you touched the switch. Now stop wasting my time with stupid lies. It's no thanks to you that you didn't commit mass murder in here. I want to know where that booby-trapped lamp came from. Who gave it to you and told you to deliver it to this station?'

Though he resisted stubbornly for a time, Leroy was no match for a hardened interrogator. Eventually he cracked and told all. It was a white man he knew as Jim who'd befriended him when he came to live in his squat. Jim had rescued him when he was about to be carved up in an alley by four National Front skinheads with big chivs. Jim had waded into all four of them single-handed and armed with nothing more than his martial arts. When he'd knocked two of them senseless with Karate blows, the survivors fled in confusion.

'He save my life, man, or I bleed to death from a cut,' said the negro, rolling up his sleeve and showing on his forearm an angry purple nine-inch long scar with horizontal stitch marks all the way down, so that it looked like some gruesome zip-fastener.

'That mother cut me real bad. The blood was pumpin' out and I thought I was gonna die. But Jim put a tourniquet on my elbow and took me to the hospital, or else I'd be dead by now. I owe him, man. You dig?'

'You don't owe anybody enough to let him use you as a murderous errand-boy, and take a whole lot of innocent lives,' said the chief inspector sternly.

Green went on to explain how he'd gone along with Jim ever since. He'd had a bad scare from the skinheads with their chivs, and he only felt safe with Jim in the unpredictable savagery of the London streets. The white man had given him money, shown him how to re-connect the electricity supply in condemned houses, and how to live off the fat of London's affluence without getting nicked by the Man. In other words Jim had helped him to enjoy a better and more enlightened way of life, so that the negro didn't like to refuse him a favour when he asked for one.

'What possible justification could he give you for planting a bomb of that power in this police station?' pursued Sperling. 'You must have known it was a highly dangerous and criminal act that could get you a long prison sentence.'

'Well, Jim he say he been getting a lot of aggravation from the Man in Highland Road. He say you don't give him no peace even in the spikes, and try to fit him up for every damn crime in the city, just because he went to his brother's funeral and the fuzz reckon he hates the Irish. He say he want to give you a lesson by settin' off a fire-cracker under your noses. But he was too well known at that nick, so he couldn't take the surprise package in himself. He ask me to do it for him.

'Man, when he tole me to go in the Highland Road nick on Saturday night when they was jumpin' about too much to know what time it was, and just leave that here bike lamp on the counter and then walk out again – and not to touch the switch, mind! – I was good and scared. I tole him I didn't want to do it. But he reckoned it was a doddle, and I still owed him one for savin' my life, as well as for the hundred quid he gave me after the Liffey Bridge job. He just made me do it, man. I guess I was scared of him. He frightened me more than the Man.'

'Tell me about the Liffey Bridge job,' said

the chief inspector softly.

'You mean you ain't sussed that yet?' said Green incredulously.

'We want your version of it, Green. How were you implicated?'

'Oh, mother! I swear to God I never knew what was going down,' wailed Green hysterically. 'He never tole me it was all a trap to blow up Mr. O'Dowd. He never let on that house was wired to go up, and all them poor people next door was gonna get killed. And now I gotta live with that, man, and Jim he couldn't care less. You gotta have casualties in a war, is all he said.'

Sperling exchanged a grim glance with Detective Sergeant Shindler.

'Are you by any chance referring to the explosion and fire in Kersey Road, Wandsworth, near the Southern Gas Depot?'

'You got it, man. Jim set that up, and roped me in to make it work. He shoulda tole me what he was goin' to do. Then I'd have split, got lost for good, and never touched his lousy hundred quid.'

'Tell me how the Liffey Bridge and Mr. O'Dowd come into it,' said the chief inspector patiently.

Leroy Green explained how he'd been coached by Jim till he was word perfect in

191

his story about how he'd met Rosyn Fitzgerald and agreed to help her to hide her cache of illicit weapons in a Wandsworth squat. He described how Jim had then taken him to the Liffey Bridge Hotel in the small hours, opened a kitchen window for him to enter, and then escorted him into the bar so that he could have a few free drinks before he was discovered there by O'Dowd.

'Did he ever tell you why he'd got it in for O'Dowd?' pursued Sperling.

'No, man. He just say he owed him one from way back, and he wanted to rowst him a bit. He never tole me he had plain murder on his mind or I wouldn't have had no part in it no way.'

'Well, you'd naturally say that now you've been caught,' said the chief inspector coldly. 'But the fact remains that you played an indispensable part in both crimes. You never came forward to tell us what you knew of the Kersey Road disaster, and then you deliberately placed an explosive device in this police station, knowing it must kill and maim people. You don't come out of all this in a very good light, Green, and you're going to rue the day you ever let this Jim talk you into anything. Can you describe him? What does he look like?'

'Just a whitey,' mumbled Green. 'All white men the same to me, man.'

'Don't give me that nonsense! How tall was he?'

"Bout an inch or two less than me.'

'Five feet ten,' nodded Sperling. 'Heavily built or slim?'

'Oh, I dunno, man. Skinny and tough is what he looked like to me.'

'Colour of hair?'

'Sandy or ginger, I think.'

'Long hair or short?'

'A square hair-cut, man. Bit like a skin-head.'

'Colour of eyes?'

'Hell, I dunno. Pale coloured, I think.'

'Good,' said Sperling. 'Now you can work with the Identikit artist to build up a like-ness of this man for us. Your co-operation might do you a bit of good when you get to court. We might give you some verbal help and make your villainy sound a bit less black than it really is.'

'We don't really need the Identikit, guv,' said Shindler. 'From what we know, I'd stake my pension it's our old client, James Montgomery Faldo, and suddenly a lot of obscure things have become crystal clear. We should have twigged it had to be a mad

S.A.S. man who caused that Kersey Street explosion: a logical continuation of his Irish vendetta to lure O'Dowd and his I.R.A. team to a booby-trapped house. By selling that bait of a weapons cache to O'Dowd, he wiped out a squad of republican sympathisers with one bomb. It was a diabolical bit of cunning to train a negro drop-out to set the trap for him.'

'It's not only the Irish he's got a vendetta against now,' said Sperling. 'He's waging one against us as well, just because we brought him in a couple of times for questioning. If I had any doubts before as to his guilt in killing O'Malley and the Roman Catholic priest, I've none now.'

'He's an outright bloody psychopath,' said Shindler. 'Whatever labels the shrinks put on him, he's certainly too mad to be left running around loose. All that know-how he's got with bombs and booby-traps and access to sophisticated detonators, it scares me to death.'

'Get a few dozen copies of his Identikit likeness run off as soon as it's completed,' said the chief inspector, 'and have them posted outside all the divisional police stations and sub-stations in South London. This man must be found quickly. In the meantime, go and interview O'Dowd at the Liffey Bridge. Get him to verify Green's story, and lean on him if you have to to make him come clean about Faldo's grudge against him. There's obviously a straight connection between O'Dowd and those three or four men from Kilburn who went to the house to recover the reported weapons. O'Dowd is not exactly smelling of roses in this matter, even though he is clean with the law. There are implications here of a conspiracy to handle arms and explosives that you might point out to O'Dowd. So let's see if we can get this bloody mess sorted.'

## TWENTY

Less than an hour later Shindler was back from Wandsworth with his report.

'Too late, guv,' he said in disgust. 'O'Dowd's flown the coop, bolted back to the Republic with his wife and family on indefinite leave. The company that owns the hotel have brought in a relief manager. They don't know when O'Dowd will be back. He went for personal and family reasons.'

'Well, I can't say that surprises me,' sighed the chief inspector. 'I reckon I'd take a powder if I knew there was a mad S.A.S. man out there, trying to blow me away. How long has O'Dowd been gone?'

'The day after the Kersey Road explosion. He knew it was meant for him. It gives strong support to Green's story. O'Dowd worked it out that he'd been set up for that booby trap by somebody who knew all about Rosyn Fitzgerald's way of life, and he wasn't hanging about to give him any more chances.'

'Well, we're going to need O'Dowd's testimony in order to get a case against Faldo,' said Sperling. 'Green's unsupported statement is just not enough for a murder trial. It might have been a different story if we'd found Faldo's prints on that booby-trapped lamp as well as Green's. But Faldo was far too fly for that. Maybe his dabs were on the detonator and battery cells, but he knew we'd never take it apart without it going off, even if we did suspect it.'

'I get your drift, guv,' said Shindler. 'With no hard evidence to lay on Faldo, the case is a non-starter. Leroy Green would be a total disaster in the witness box when some sharp defence brief got at him. He's none too bright, and could be trapped into telling about three contradictory sets of lies in as many minutes.'

'Our main difficulty with Green as a witness is that he's black and Faldo's white, so that this whole case is shot through with racial undertones and overtones. The brief defending Faldo would exploit that to the full. At a time when all these hot-gospelling black militants are determined to have the blood of some white racist for the Wandsworth house fire disaster, Leroy Green could easily be smeared as having been leaned on by black extremists and made to finger Faldo as the culprit. Faldo is white, and Faldo is S.A.S., so where would they find a more convincing scapegoat for the bombing in Kersey Road? This racial prejudice cuts both ways, you know. The blacks have got as much of it as we have, and they use it in a more self-righteous way, which tends to get up the noses of the indigenous natives. At the first insinuation of Leroy Green being subjected to undue influence and pressure by black extremists, all his credibility as a witness, supposing he ever had any, will evaporate. It could be made to argue for Faldo's innocence in a big way by a clever barrister out for glory in a murder trial, showing how Faldo, the honourable soldier, was being thrown to the wolves on the evidence of one man, a black, merely to satisfy the vindictiveness of black ideologues.'

'It's a bugger, isn't it?' agreed Shindler.

'The law can no longer take its uninterrupted course because race relations get in the way. That's why we must have O'Dowd's supportive testimony as the bed-rock of our case against Faldo. There's only one thing for it, Shindler. You'll have to go across to Ireland and get a full statement from O'Dowd. If it tallies substantially with Green's account, your next task will be to persuade O'Dowd to come back here as our principal witness against Faldo.'

'Would you blame him if he didn't want to come, guv?'

'I don't really see what he's got to be scared of when once we've got Faldo in custody. Anyway he must want to come back to his job as manager at the Liffey Bridge when he knows he's not in danger. He's obviously not the type to want to rot in an Irish bog for the rest of his life. I'll get in touch with the Garda, put our problem to them, and ask them to trace O'Dowd's present whereabouts for us.'

Three days later, having received precise information from the Dublin police on O'Dowd's whereabouts, Detective Sergeant Shindler boarded an Aer Lingus jet at Heathrow, and landed at Dublin Airport in the rain. He was taken by taxi to Garda H.Q. where he showed his credentials and introduced himself to Superintendent Wade, who'd handled the O'Dowd enquiry at the Dublin end.

Wade was a tall, rangy C.I.D. man who had the unmistakable air of a senior police-man with thirty years' service. He had sunken, sallow cheeks, rheumy eyes and a bitter mouth, and a hair-line advancing erratically up his skull. He also had a chain-smoking problem that made his clothes reek like an old ashtray.

Wade immediately recognised Shindler as one of his own kind who didn't use kid gloves in getting what he wanted from suspects, so he was going to need close supervision. With his jaundiced view of the English, Wade was suspicious at first that the paranoid London police were trying to start extradition proceedings against one of his countrymen because of some suspected involvement with the I.R.A., and he wasn't going along with it.

Shindler had to explain the situation all over again, stage by stage, laying stress on the fact that the real enemy was a mad S.A.S. man in London, who was going about blowing people up, and O'Dowd's evidence was sorely needed to build up a case against him.

'Just give me his address,' said Shindler smoothly, 'and I'll go and get his statement. It's only a straightforward verification of something we know already.'

'Well, I'm thinking I'll be coming with you, just to see you don't lean on him too hard, getting statements he wouldn't want to be making,' growled Wade distrustfully. 'Now he's on his own soil he's entitled to all our protection, so he is.'

He telephoned for his car, a large black Ford Ghia with a uniformed Garda man as driver, and sat side by side with Shindler in the tobacco-reeking back seat as they drove through the southern outskirts of Dublin along the main road through the Wicklow hills leading to Kilkenny.

In the intensely green rain-swept country-side, they turned off down a muddy side road which led through dripping woods to the sprawling village of Monoghan with its white, single-storey cottages, its several pubs and its imposing neo-Gothic Catholic church. A mile beyond Monoghan in the real wilderness was the large family farm-house, where four generations of fast-breeding O'Dowds all lived together, rapidly getting fat on E.E.C. farm subsidies. In order to make room in an emergency for Donald O'Dowd, his wife and all his children descending on them from London, the O'Dowds had just moved up and squashed in closer as in all rabbit warrens.

When the police car splashed into the farmyard, Donald O'Dowd had just come back from the pub and was loafing in the huge farmhouse kitchen in a rocking chair before a large open fire of smouldering peat. He was in his shirt-sleeves, and his big belly bulged over his brass belt buckle. Cigar smoke from the inevitable Havana wreathed about his head. His wife Sile was washing endless dishes at the sink, while one of his sisters-in-law ironed a huge pile of laundry on the broad kitchen table. Numerous O'Dowd offspring gambolled and squabbled noisily underfoot.

'Ah, Mr. O'Dowd from London, is it not?' said Superintendent Wade genially as he displayed his credentials. 'I'm Superintendent

Wade of the Garda, and this gentleman is Detective Sergeant Shindler of the London Metropolitan Police. He'll be wanting to ask you some questions, I'm thinking, and I'm here to protect your rights as an Irish citizen in his own country, so I am. You don't have to answer a word to this officer unless you chose to do so. That's your privilege.'

As he recognised Shindler, O'Dowd snapped into startled awareness out of his beery stupor, and his big red face lost a lot of its colour. He looked like a man face to face with the reality of his worst dream.

'We've already met at the Liffey Bridge Hotel in Wandsworth,' said Shindler curtly. 'Some time ago, Mr. O'Dowd, you may remember, I came to talk to you about an employee and countrywoman of yours, Rosyn Fitzgerald, who was brutally murdered on Wandsworth Common.'

'To be sure, I remember it,' muttered O'Dowd. 'A shocking wicked crime, so it was. Is it news of her killer you're bringing me?'

'Not specifically. But we certainly haven't closed the file on the case.'

'Then how can I be helping you any more, Officer? I told you all I knew about her in London. I can't tell you more now you've followed me over the water.'

'This visit is to do with a different line of enquiry,' said Shindler. 'What dealings have you ever had with a man called James Faldo of the S.A.S. Regiment, formerly operational in Northern Ireland, and known to us as the mad bomber?'

'Holy Mary!' spluttered O'Dowd, turning paler. 'Why would I have dealings with such a man? I never met him and wouldn't know him if I did, and that's the gospel truth.'

'In that case why would he want to kill you?' demanded Shindler bluntly.

'That I don't know, and it's certainly news to me that he does.'

'Come off it, Mr. O'Dowd. Isn't the danger from Faldo the reason why you suddenly took off like a scalded cat, left your London job as a hotel manager, and bolted home to the Republic with all your family?'

'No, it is not,' protested O'Dowd indignantly. 'Since you're askin', I took a wee holiday for my family's sake, purely health reasons, so it was. Mrs O'Dowd was feeling run down with all the pressures of the Liffey Bridge, and the children needed some fresh country air to put the colour in their cheeks again. Isn't that reason enough for coming here?'

'I don't believe it's the right reason,' said Shindler doggedly. 'In view of the sworn statement of Leroy Green, a West Indian youth whom you know very well, I think you bolted in a panic from London because you believed with good reason that your life and your family's safety were menaced by this Faldo. And I don't blame you.'

He related the stark facts of Leroy Green's statement about the events leading up to the disastrous explosion in the condemned house in Wandsworth, while O'Dowd's big bleary eyes grew wider with horror.

''Tis lies! 'Tis all dirty lies!' he interjected vehemently. Even Superintendent Wade was hushed into silence by Shindler's narrative.

'Faldo set you up to get killed in that booby-trapped house with his lies about a haul of weapons hidden there, and we'd very much like to know what grudge he'd got against you.'

'Sure I know nothing at all of any grudge.'

'But you didn't fall for it, did you?' went on Shindler implacably. 'You didn't go yourself to collect Rosyn Fitzgerald's alleged arms cache, as Faldo intended. You tipped off some hard men in Kilburn to recover them, and they got killed instead. It was your duty as a law-abiding citizen to inform the police about the hidden weapons, and let them handle it. But instead you conspired with others to move the arms illegally, presumably for future use by terrorists in your republican cause.'

'Indeed I did not!' protested O'Dowd desperately. 'You're building me up to be the villain I'm not, and you're completely wrong.'

'I don't think so. It's logical deduction based on the information supplied by the West Indian, Leroy Green. I think I ought to point out where your action places you in the eyes of English law. You conspired with others, now unfortunately dead, to handle arms and explosives concealed by Rosyn Fitzgerald in an empty house. So if you should ever wish to return to England, that's the charge you'll have to face: conspiracy to handle explosives. And in the current climate of anti-terrorist hysteria the custodial sentences are heavy, particularly in view of the serious loss of life caused by the explosives you were dabbling with. However, if you should see fit to co-operate with us by telling all you know about James Faldo and why he's waging a murderous personal vendetta against you—'

'Ah,' interposed Superintendent Wade,

'the *quid pro quo,* is it not?'

'In return for your help in building up a convincing indictment against Faldo,' continued Shindler, 'I'm sure my guv'nor would be prepared to leave out the explosives charge that's hanging over you. Then, with Faldo put away for good, you'd have nothing to fear. You could return to your normal civilised life minding your hotel in Wandsworth.'

O'Dowd had gone a ghastly pale colour at the realisation of the deadly quandary he was in.

'It's bloody diabolical, so it is!' he exclaimed. 'I can't tell you anything at all about this man Faldo. I know nothing about him except what you've told me here, that he's a member of the S.A.S. and wants to blow people up. But now you're trying to blackmail me, so you are, demanding information that I don't possess, under threat of prosecution on some trumped-up explosives charge when I get back to London. You're acting like God Almighty, threatening to keep me away from my job in London for ever, unless I tell you what you want to hear about some murdering English sojer who's got up your nose. Sure I reckon the English Law Society and the Civil

Rights people over in England would like to be hearing about your technique with witnesses.'

'Wait a bit! Wait a bit!' interrupted the Garda superintendent, who'd been listening avidly to the whole dialogue. 'It's true you're being a bit rough on Mr. O'Dowd, Sergeant, so you are. And I don't think you have real cause to be, or are going to get anywhere by it. Now the way I'm understanding the case, the only incriminating information you London police have so far about your mad bomber, Faldo, is the cock-and-bull story that you've managed to extort from some West Indian feller with a long record of petty crime. Sure, and a really reliable, truthful witness he sounds like! Correct me if I'm not right so far, Sergeant.'

'You're definitely wrong about the cock-and-bull part,' replied Shindler angrily. 'The booby-trapped bike lamp that nearly blew up my station was real enough, and Green was the one who delivered it. We can charge him with it, but we really want the man who constructed the bomb and got Green to deliver it: Faldo. Apart from the bike lamp episode, Green's statement fits a lot of apparently unrelated facts and brings them together in a convincing pattern to fit the events. We're pretty sure that if he wanted to, Mr. O'Dowd could verify Green's statement and nail Faldo for booby-trapping a house that killed more than a dozen people.'

'And that's why you're here, to be sure, Sergeant,' declared Superintendent Wade triumphantly. 'You need another witness to confirm Green's testimony. In itself it's not enough for a court of law. Your chief inspector admitted as much when he spoke to me on the telephone about the urgency of finding and interviewing Mr. O'Dowd.

'Now, correct me if I'm wrong, Sergeant. But if you need an independent witness to corroborate Green's statement on Faldo, you also need an independent witness to confirm all the wicked lies that this Green feller told you about his midnight visit to Mr. O'Dowd, and taking an army hand grenade to prove to him that Rosyn Fitz-gerald's store of arms was no moonshine.

'So where is that army hand grenade now then, Sergeant? Shouldn't you be able to produce it to corroborate Green's story, if there's a shred of truth in it?'

'It never existed. It did not!' declared O'Dowd fervently. 'And this Leroy Green was lying in his teeth if he says he ever came to me with a story of weapons that were hidden by Rosyn Fitzgerald. I never met that West Indian feller in my life, and that's the gospel truth.'

'And I suppose it's all lies and moonshine that a booby-trapped house in Wandsworth was blown up with heavy loss of life to the Asian squatters next door,' retorted Shindler bitterly.

'Hard men from Kilburn did that. You said so yourself,' said Superintendent Wade complacently. 'And all dead, so they are, so who can ever know what they were up to? What evidence do you have to connect them with Mr. O'Dowd? Face up to it, Sergeant. You came here to get supportive evidence against Faldo to charge him with these crimes. To serve your purpose you were prepared to threaten Mr. O'Dowd with a conspiracy charge. Handling explosives, you said he was, on the testimony of a West Indian tearaway, when all the time you had no more corroborative evidence for Green's story about Mr. O'Dowd than you had for Green's story about Faldo. Sure you're a regular wizard with words, so you are, Sergeant. But words are all you'll be having to go on, I'm thinking. Mr. O'Dowd can't give you the corroboration you need on Faldo. Nor can he confirm the charge against himself that you'd like to be pressing him with. So perhaps we'd better be getting back to Dublin now, and not waste any more of the good man's time.'

O'Dowd was smiling broadly at Shindler's discomfiture, and his broad red face had returned to its natural colour.

'No hard feelings, Sergeant,' he said magnanimously, 'none whatsoever. When all this is over you'll always be welcome to drop in for a yarn and a bevy on the house at the Liffey Bridge. And now what'll you be saying to a wee dram of Irish to warm the cockles for your long flight back to London, eh?'

He crossed the kitchen to a large, ornately carved corner cupboard of dark oak, and produced three glass tumblers and a bottle of Irish whisky three-quarters full.

'Sure, and that's very civil of you, Mr. O'Dowd,' said Superintendent Wade, stubbing out his cigarette in anticipation. 'Very civil indeed, so it is.'

# TWENTY-ONE

When Shindler arrived back in London from his abortive journey, he was still fuming over the way he'd been outmanoeuvred, frustrated and fooled by the soft-talking Irish. As he made his report verbally to Detective Chief Inspector Sperling, he could tell by the irritated pursing of lips and the abrasive rasp in the voice that Sperling considered he'd bungled it.

'I'm absolutely sure that smarmy bugger O'Dowd was lying in his teeth,' swore Shindler viciously. 'I've questioned too many suspects not to get the vibes when a guilty man is covering up something he can't afford to let us know. I believe Leroy Green's story about the midnight visit to the Liffey Bridge and the hand grenade for authenticity is substantially correct. O'Dowd tipped off those thick shamuses in Kilburn to go and recover the arms, because he's a long-standing I.R.A. sympathiser. Faldo had him taped, and that's why he was out to kill him. It all adds up right. But O'Dowd daren't admit to knowing why Faldo was after him, because then he'd have to give us the reason, which must be some skulduggery connected with acts of I.R.A. terrorism in this country. If it came to light, O'Dowd could be permanently excluded from this country under the Prevention of Terrorism Act.'

'But this is all conjecture,' said Sperling impatiently. 'Green's unsupported testimony is not enough, and you couldn't get confirmation for it, could you?'

'I reckon I could have sweated it out of him if that bloody Garda superintendent hadn't insisted on being there,' growled Shindler. 'But he was just rooting for O'Dowd, gave him every support and encouragement in withholding information, and showed him how to weasel his way out of the trap I thought I'd got him in.'

'So we'll have to wait till O'Dowd comes back here and is outside Garda protection.'

'That won't be till he knows Faldo is either dead or locked up for good,' said Shindler in disgust. 'The big fat bugger is good on self-preservation, and he's really cosy in that big farmhouse out in the rolling bogs with his home-made fire-water. He's in no hurry to come back, so what can we do?'

'We can step up the hunt for Faldo,' retorted Sperling. 'While he's running loose out there, lives are in danger. There could be other London republicans on his hit list, not to mention his paranoid hatred towards this police station. Next time he tries to blow us up it could be a bigger and better bomb, and we might not be so lucky as to spot it in time. I would think that Faldo must be getting short of money before much longer. Then he'll either have to steal in order to eat, or go to work to earn money. In either case it should bring him within our range. According to his army record, at his advanced training unit he did a course on vehicle maintenance, and he has the standard army qualification of a trained motor mechanic. So if he does decide to work for living, he'll be in some garage or workshop, mending motors. We'll have the information circulated together with his picture.'

'And what do we do when we find him, guv? We still haven't got enough on him to make a case.'

'Let's face that problem when we get there,' said the chief inspector. 'We could try to get him to a shrink, and have him detained for his own protection pending psychiatric tests. The important thing is to

get him off the streets and keep him somewhere separated from his haul of explosives.
We just need to keep a friendly eye on him
so that he doesn't set up any more booby-
traps or murder any more Irish. And that's
something else we ought to be working on:
the discovery of Faldo's store of explosives
and detonators. He must have brought them
with him from Ulster, stolen from army
ordnance, or looted from captured I.R.A.
bomb-making factories.

'The point is, he's kept it hidden successfully all the time he's been in London, living
rough in spikes and squats, and he's always
been able to put his hand on it when he
needed it for some bloody outrage. If we
could just find one packet of plastic or one
detonator with Faldo's dabs on it, it would
go a hell of a long way towards convicting
him. There are precedents with several
I.R.A. bombers who've been stitched up
and put away for having just one hand-print
on an explosive device. Any ideas about
getting that evidence, Sergeant?'

'When I think of all the derelict warehouses and condemned houses, the cellars,
broken drains and culverts within the five-
mile radius that Faldo's been moving about
in, the needle in the field of haystacks looks

like a simple proposition,' said Shindler disconsolately.

'Aren't you overlooking something in your dedicated pessimism?' said Sperling impatiently. 'What about Leroy Green? He's admitted to sharing squats with Faldo, and became his faithful Uncle Tom nigger after Faldo rescued him from a knife attack and saved his life. It's too much to expect Faldo would have taken Green into his confidence about where he kept the explosives hidden, but at least Green should be able to take us to the places where he camped with Faldo, the squats he shared with him, especially at the time when Faldo was planning the Kersey Street explosion and fixing us his booby-trap bike lamp for our benefit. Once we know his dossing places, we can search all the buildings and cellars and drains within a certain radius of them. Using dogs trained to sniff out explosives, we might get lucky.'

'O.K., guv. I'll get it set up,' said Shindler. 'It's a pretty long shot, but I suppose there's always the chance that Green might have noticed a bit more than Faldo gave him credit for. With all he's got stacked against him, he should be only too glad to co-operate. He's as miserable as hell in Brixton, and being driven round on a panoramic tour of all his old hunting grounds might stimulate his grey matter very productively. What about man-power, guv? We could do with the whole metropolitan force on this.'

'Just locate the places where Faldo went to ground while he was with Green. We'll lay on the search parties afterwards.'

So Detective Sergeant Shindler accompanied by Detective Constable Neilson went to the Remand Wing at Brixton Prison and signed out Leroy Green into their custody. They explained to him their current thinking on Faldo's store of explosives, and told him it had to be found. Leroy was eager to co-operate, in the touching belief that his help might go some way towards reducing his custodial sentence when he was eventually convicted. But he was positive he'd never once seen Jim humping a sackful of arms and explosives about.

'Dunno where he kept his gear at,' said Leroy vaguely. 'But he sure as hell don't want me to sus it. When he shoved off on his own, I wasn't goin' snoopin' on him no way, man. He was a scary kind of dude and didn't trust nobody.'

However, Leroy had a sound detailed knowledge of the slums where he'd been brought up, and a pretty clear memory of the places he'd stayed in while he was going around with Jim.

'Jim wouldn't sleep in no cellar,' he informed them. 'Reckoned he was in a trap there, you dig? Always had to have a back way out where he could split fast. He liked the ground floor of a house, but only if there was no other dudes in it.'

Leroy took the detectives to decaying houses, old disused factories and crumbling warehouses from Brockley to New Cross, from Camberwell to Clapham, and pointed out the bleak Spartan shelters where Faldo had dossed down in his sleeping bag. As he didn't reckon to spend more than two nights in the same place, the little red flags on the street map pinned up in the chief inspector's office that marked Faldo's trail increased at an alarming rate.

With all the manpower that could be mustered, and assisted by tracker dogs trained to sniff out explosives, the police carried out a painstaking search of empty houses, factories and drains in the neighbourhood of every site where Faldo had pitched his camp. Their only success, which marked the end of the search and a decisive failure, was the discovery of Faldo's empty army kitbag.

It had been trodden into the rubble under an old factory wall and located there by an eager police alsation. Though heavily plastered with dirt and brick dust they could still read the stencilled insignia on the canvas: 1483594 Sergt. J.M. Faldo.

Whether it had been finally emptied of its contents and abandoned there by Faldo himself, or whether it had been discovered in its hiding place and pillaged by scavengers, dossers or children, there was no means of knowing. Nobody was ever going to admit to finding a few live hand grenades or pistols and ammunition, for which there was always a ready and lucrative market in the underworld.

## TWENTY-TWO

Some weeks afterwards, a detective from another division, following up an enquiry into a stolen car that had been used in a robbery, called at a small garage in Balham, a boarded-in shelter under one of the arches of a railway viaduct. Here an old lag known to the police as Fred (the Weasel) Whitlam ran his motor repair and respraying business just on the right side of the law.

Having asked his routine questions of Fred Whitlam, who was as innocent as the new-born day and could give him no help whatsoever, the detective turned disconsolately away. But on leaving the office, out of the corner of his eye he noticed that Fred Whitlam had an assistant working busily in a far corner of the garage on welding the sub-frame of a beat-up old Mini.

For a brief moment the welder's eye-shield was lowered as he adjusted the valve on the acetylene cylinder, and the keen-eyed detective caught a glimpse of the worker's face, lit up luridly in the blue flame of the burner. He knew he'd seen the face before somewhere, probably in the ever-shifting rogues' gallery of pictures circulated by Scotland Yard of men wanted for questioning. But he gave no sign of interest or recognition as he walked away. He went casually off down the grotty street in the shadow of the viaduct, and before he turned the corner he remembered with quickening excitement where that welder's face belonged. It was Sergeant Faldo, the mad bomber, who'd tried to blow up the Highland Road nick with a murderous booby-trap and was urgently wanted by Catford C.I.D.

An hour later in response to the windfall information, Detective Sergeant Shindler and Detective Constable Neilson drew a .38 Smith and Wesson revolver apiece from the station armoury in preparation for bringing in the mad bomber. Knowing his record, they were prepared for anything, and they meant to nail him down, dead or alive.

'Don't shoot him unless he leaves you no other choice,' admonished the chief inspector, 'and don't let him get in touch with his brief. The longer we can keep him incommunicado, the more chance we'll have of screwing a confession out of him. And the safer we'll all be.'

Approaching unnoticed, the two detectives rushed quickly into the viaduct garage where Faldo, dressed in greasy blue overalls with an old black army beret on his head, was still working conscientiously on the Mini. He looked up to see the two menacing figures hemming him in, and climbed slowly to his feet with a large ring spanner in his hand. The expression on his face was one of smouldering resentment and contempt as he looked from one to the other of his old enemies who'd first arrested him at a funeral. But he watched them warily without any attempt to make a break for it, as if he knew what each man was gripping inside his coat pocket.

'So it's Abbott and Costello still doing a comic turn,' he growled. 'Don't you sods every try to catch vandals and muggers and clean up the bloody streets a bit? You're only bothered about the easy pinch to make it look good on your books.'

'You're under arrest, Faldo,' said Shindler grimly. 'You don't have to say anything, but what you do say will be written down and used against you.'

Swiftly he took out a set of handcuffs, clipped one bracelet on his own wrist, and snapped the other on Faldo's, so that any move to resist was effectively pre-empted.

'The car is round the corner,' he said, 'and we'd rather you walked there than have to be carried.'

'What the bloody hell do you think you're doing?' snarled Faldo. 'You can't get away with your Gestapo technique in this country. What am I charged with anyway?'

'That'll be put to you at the Station.'

'Well, I want to ring my brief.'

'All in good time.'

'I'm allowed to make one phone call on being arrested. I want to make it now.'

'You'll make it from the Station.'

'You hear that, Fred?' said Faldo to the garage owner, who was witnessing the drama with dismay from his plywood-panelled office. 'These buggers are pulling a fast one, trying to hijack me to their nick, and denying me my human rights. Do me a favour. Get on the phone to my brief, Mr. Betts of New Cross – his number's in the book – and tell him Jim Faldo's being hounded and harassed by the fuzz again. It's the Catford lot. They're all bloody mad. They've been trying to get me on one trumped-up charge after another ever since I arrived in London. Tell Mr. Betts. Once they get me down in the cellar at Gestapo Headquarters, God knows what they'll do to get a confession unless Mr. Betts gets there fast to make them obey the law.'

'Leave it out and mind your own bloody business,' hissed Neilson menacingly to Fred Whitlam. 'This is Faldo, the mad bomber, wanted for mass murder. If you stick your hooter in, getting involved on his side, we'll know what to do about looking into your little piece of action, won't we?'

'Come away and keep your trap shut, you daft bugger!' whispered Shindler to his over-zealous colleague. 'Haven't we got enough problems doing our job without you giving live ammunition to the bent lawyers to shoot our arses off?'

He dragged Faldo unceremoniously by the wrist out of the garage and into the back of their car, while Neilson got behind the wheel and took off at high speed for Catford.

At the police station Faldo was placed in an interview room under guard, and Detective Chief Inspector Sperling, accompanied by Shindler, lost no time in coming to interrogate him. After cautioning him again, the chief inspector began with the affair of the booby-trapped bicycle lamp, and read him Leroy Green's confession.

'We believe Green to be telling the truth,' said Sperling. 'He'd never have the imagination to concoct all this out of malice towards you. And he certainly wouldn't have been able to put that sophisticated booby-trap together himself.'

But Faldo remained ice-cold and indifferent to the accusations, as if he'd switched himself off permanently from all his alleged crimes and was confident of never being convicted.

'Green says one thing, and I say he's lying,' declared Faldo flatly. 'His word against mine. You'll have to do better than that to prove I made the booby-trap.'

'Are you denying that you ever knew Leroy Green?'

'Of course not. It's true what he says that I rescued him from some skinheads, and got him to hospital when he was bleeding to death from a knife-cut. We shared a squat a few times, and I helped him out, the poor incompetent bugger! And then he drifted off somewhere the way these no-hopers do, and I never saw him again.'

'You didn't quarrel with him?'

'Of course not. We didn't have enough in common to quarrel about anything.'

'In that case, why would he try to land you in trouble by saying it was you who gave him the bomb and bribed him to deliver it here?'

'Oh, Christ!' exclaimed Faldo in disgust. 'Isn't it obvious? When you'd nailed him and frightened the pants off him, he was ready to say anything to please you. And as he knew I'd been in the army in Ireland, I was the likeliest customer he could think of to put the blame on. He had to come up with a name, or you'd have thumped one out of him, wouldn't you?'

'Is that the best you can do, Faldo, in view of the other crimes of violence you're suspected of?' said the chief inspector scathingly.

'All right. You want another reason why Green put me in the frame? Try this one: The bastard who tried to blow you up and used Leroy Green as his errand-boy pretended to be me. He gave my name to Green because I was known to be ex-S.A.S., and once you'd got my name you wouldn't waste time looking for anybody else because I had the know-how to make bombs that would work. Isn't that how it stacks up?'

'I'd be willing enough to buy that explanation, Faldo, if it wasn't for all your other horrifying crimes of violence.'

'What crimes? You've persecuted me, tried to make me feel I'm not a member of the human race, and all for what? My crimes are just in your head, or you'd be charging me by now.'

'We'll charge you in the end, don't worry. You came to London after your army discharge with the express purpose of paying off old scores against a couple of notorious Ulster republicans. And you paid them in full. Then there was that shocking affair of the Roman Catholic priest in Camberwell being maltreated till he died. Most horrifying of all was the trap you set for O'Dowd

225

of the Liffey Bridge Hotel with a load of explosives in a condemned house in Wandsworth. Your overkill caused the house next door to go up and kill all those Asian squatters, and we're still getting a lot of flak from that over the racial issue.'

'My heart bleeds for you,' retorted Faldo. 'What evidence do you have that that affair was down to me?'

'The testimony of Leroy Green: how you gave him a hundred quid to go and tell some tale of an arms dump to O'Dowd, knowing full well he was an old republican sympathiser with a lot of crazier republican friends in London, and couldn't resist a windfall of weapons coming his way. You even gave Green a 36 grenade, ready primed, to give credence to his story. You coached him till he was word perfect in some cock-and-bull story of how he was befriended by Rosyn Fitzgerald, and had hidden the weapons for her in his squat because he owed her. Then you took Green to the Liffey Bridge Hotel in the middle of the night and forced a way in for him so that he could talk to O'Dowd without witnesses. All this is in Green's sworn statement, which will be part of the indictment against you.'

'Like I said before, his word against mine,'

retorted Faldo still unruffled. 'You won't convict me of capital crimes just on the say-so of a poor demented nig-nog, who you've probably told what to say or else.'

'O'Dowd of the Liffey Bridge will confirm Green's testimony,' said the chief inspector, tight-lipped. 'No jury will ever believe that two such widely different characters conspired against you with a story that tallies in every detail, and is supported by such momentous events as the Kersey Street explosion and the delivery of a murderous booby-trap to this station.'

'Hard luck! O'Dowd's buggered off,' retorted Faldo casually. 'Probably skulking in the Republic. You won't see his arse for dust.'

'How do you know that?'

'Wouldn't you have buggered off in his position? He knows he can't confirm Green's story without dropping himself in it up to the neck for conspiring with the I.R.A. to handle weapons and explosives. And you'd be leaning on him all the time to help you stitch me up, regardless of what happened to him. No wonder he got lost. If I was him I'd stay lost.'

'Look,' said Sperling, swallowing his anger and frustration with difficulty, 'you may not realise it, Faldo, but you're a very sick man.

You need rest and proper treatment over a long period to keep you from destroying yourself. I'm prepared to admit that you're a victim, too, in some respects. The horrifying circumstances of your brother and his wife being killed in their home by terrorists would be enough to unhinge anybody's sanity. And then there have been the appalling conditions of difficulty and danger under which you've worked for so long in Northern Ireland. You're entitled to call in the experts and take advantage of the best treatment available. If you'll give your consent I can arrange for you to be seen by a consultant psychiatrist, and he'll prescribe treatment according to your needs. You can have a good long rest in ideal conditions for as long as it takes to get you well again.'

'Thanks very much, Inspector,' said Faldo, greatly amused. 'You mean the writ of *Habeas Corpus* doesn't run in the padded cell, and it's a way of getting me shut away indefinitely, with slimy, soft-talking shrinks pumping me full of dope till I really do go mad. In order to get out of there I'd have to be just as barmy and twice as cunning as the shrinks. It's a good offer, Inspector, but I don't think I'll take it. I'd rather take my chance with the criminal law than venture into the jungle of the dope-pushers and mind-benders, especially as you've got no case against me.'

'For God's sake, get him back to his cell!' swore the chief inspector, stalking out in a fury.

## TWENTY-THREE

Later that afternoon, the criminal's lawyer, Joshua Betts, who'd been tipped off about Faldo's arrest, arrived at the Highland Road Police Station demanding access to his client. After a long discussion with Faldo in his cell, the little gnome-like lawyer, bristling with indignation, was demanding to see the chief inspector. He was shown into Sperling's office and took up his inquisitorial stance as if he were berating a hostile witness in a court of law.

'May I ask the nature of the charges you're preferring against my client?' he demanded truculently.

'No secret about that,' retorted Sperling. 'In the first instance we're charging him with handling explosives and conspiring to bring a bomb into this police station with intent to endanger life. There will be other charges, of course, and I'm sending the papers to the Director of Public Prosecutions. I shall need his instructions before proceeding.'

'I see,' said Betts ominously. 'I understand that the indictment for sending the bomb here depends on the testimony of a single witness, a young tearaway called Leroy Green, and that there's no other supportive evidence?'

'That is so.'

'My client absolutely refutes Green's testimony and denies the charge.'

'Of course he does.'

'But you know as well as I do, Chief Inspector, one man's unsupported evidence is not enough for securing a conviction on a serious charge, particularly if the witness has Green's criminal record and stands discredited before he enters the witness box. Even if the magistrates order a committal, no jury in the Central Criminal Court would ever convict. It's a waste of public money to proceed with these charges.'

'You would say that, of course!'

'I certainly would! And it's obvious to everyone that you badly need a scapegoat for the Kersey Street bomb outrage, so that you can convince the distraught coloured communities of the grand impartial efficiency of the London police. The ethnic minority leaders are baying for blood over all those dead squatters. Faldo is your only suspect – a conveniently white suspect – so you'll move heaven and earth to fasten the responsibility on him, merely as a fence-mending job on London's race relations.'

'That's a bloody cheap, contemptible allegation,' exclaimed the chief inspector furiously.

'Nevertheless, it's what an awful lot of observant and discerning people will be saying if this case ever comes to court on the existing evidence,' countered Betts. 'In the meantime I want my client released on bail under the terms of the 1980 Bail Act.'

'I'm sorry,' said Sperling stubbornly, 'I can't release Faldo from custody, and if I have to I'll fight you on it all the way up to the Lord Chief Justice.'

'May I ask why? Faldo has no criminal record. If he had a long list of arrests and convictions for crimes of violence, I could understand your strongly bigoted fear of him.'

'He may not be in the computer at

C.R.O.,' retorted Sperling grimly, 'but I've seen his army record book. Before he joined the S.A.S. he was twice court-martialled and demoted in rank for acts of violence against republican Irish.'

'His natural and admitted enemies, of course. Wasn't that the job he was being paid to do at the time? Who but the overpoweringly self-righteous can really determine the dividing line between the correct path of duty and the exuberance of over-enthusiasm or over-reaction?'

'You can put what label you like on him, but I know a really dangerous man when I see one. If Faldo goes free I'm afraid of another and perhaps successful attempt to blow up this police station.'

'What absolute rubbish!'

'The man's a dangerous psychopath, and everybody needs protecting from him.'

'Really, Chief Inspector! Are you qualified to make that kind of judgement?'

'Certainly I am, when my own life may be at risk, and I know what this man can do.'

'You mean you *suspect* what this man can do,' said Betts disagreeably. 'If we're to bandy psychiatric jargon about, I'm probably nearer the truth in saying that you're paranoid about this man. It's become a test of your virility to get the better of him.'

'Look here, Mr. Betts, if you really want to help Faldo, why don't you persuade him to submit himself to psychiatric examination and a course of treatment?'

'Why should I do that when the man is as sane as you or I? He told me what you were up to – to get him put away at all costs, with or without a conviction – and he's determined to resist it. Only a magistrate can order him to be remanded for reports when he comes before the courts. In the meantime I shall seek an injunction to have him released on bail.'

'Last time you wheeled and dealed for Faldo's release against our wishes, it cost the lives of more than a dozen people,' said Sperling bitterly. 'But then, people like you always know what's best for everybody.'

'And your diagnosis on what's best for everybody is that they should all be locked up, of course,' snarled the gnome ill-naturedly as he hobbled away.

Quicker than had been anticipated the advice came back from the Director of Public Prosecutions. It stated forthrightly that the charge of planting an explosive device in the Highland Road Police Station was well substantiated against Leroy Green by his own admission as well as by the evidence of his finger-prints on the lamp. The case against him was to be proceeded with.

But as there was no *prima facie* evidence against the suspect James Faldo of having been implicated, the case against him was unproven. The verbal evidence of Green on its own was highly suspect. Similarly Green's unsupported evidence that he was used by Faldo to lure Donald O'Dowd to a booby-trapped house in Wandsworth must also fail for lack of support. Defending Counsel would drive a horse and cart through the prosecution's case and have it laughed out of court, even assuming that Green, the sole witness, didn't change his story under hostile cross-examination and admit that he'd told a pack of lies under pressure from black militants.

With no viable charge against Faldo, he should be set free forthwith.

Detective Chief Inspector Sperling realised with a kind of world-weary bitterness that he'd lost his battle. The system of checks and balances laboriously designed to safeguard the criminal had once again proved too effective to stop a policeman doing what was necessary to safeguard society.

Sperling picked up the telephone and asked for Faldo to be brought up from the cells to his office.

The ex-soldier came in, still wearing the greasy overalls he'd had on when he was arrested, but washed and shaved with that air of crisp alertness which he'd fostered all through his professional life.

'What now then?' he began suspiciously. 'Have you dreamed up another charge, or coerced another phoney witness to swear my life away?'

'No, Faldo,' sighed the chief inspector. 'I did my best to stop your antics, but I've been over-ruled by those who know better. The D.P.P. will only advise prosecution when there's a better than fifty-fifty chance of getting a conviction. In your case there's no such chance. By a combination of your infernal good luck and diabolical cunning, there's insufficient evidence to charge you with any of those serious crimes we all know you committed, so you're free to go.'

'What!' exclaimed Faldo incredulously. 'Just like that? After all the bullying and harassment you've put me through, you really acknowledge my innocence at last? Is that what you're saying?'

'No, it's not what I'm saying at all. I'm saying I can't get enough hard evidence to stitch you up for any of the crimes that you and I know you committed in London during the past few weeks. But of course, if you'd like to make a full confession of all the horrific things you've done to various people since you arrived here from Ulster, I'll be only too glad to take it to the D.P.P. and inform him that we now have a case.'

'You never give up hope, do you?' said Faldo with a sardonic grin. 'Even though it is only in your mind. Full marks for being a trier, Inspector.'

'Just do me one favour, will you?' said the chief inspector. 'Get right away from my manor and don't ever come back. If you stay here you're going to have one of my men on your tail right round the clock, reporting on your every move, just to make sure you don't pass any more bombs over the counter.'

'And what do you consider to be your manor? Where do you draw the demarcation line?'

'Anywhere in London is my manor as far as you're concerned. Just remember that O'Dowd will be coming back to the Liffey

236

Bridge when he gets pissed off with the rainy bogs, and we might just persuade him to confirm Leroy Green's allegations about the cunning trap you set to blow O'Dowd up in Kersey Street.'

'Don't worry,' replied Faldo. 'There's nothing in London to make me want to stay here. I've always known I shall have to get back into that old war again.'

'You mean re-enlist?'

'Not bloody likely. Not to have to fight with one arm tied behind my back, and get court-martialled on the say-so of some lying, bloodthirsty mick. I mean as a free-lance, fighting my own war under cover.'

'I'm not with you.'

'You don't have to be. I shall probably nip across to the Republic and join the mob that blew up Airey Neave at the House of Commons, the Irish National Liberation Army. When I've done a few explosives jobs for them and got them to trust me, I'll be able to knock off all their big wheels from the inside.'

'And when they sus you, you'll meet a worse fate than that other gung-ho warrior who tried to take on the I.R.A. single-handed. Captain Nairac, wasn't it?'

'Why should they sus me?' said Faldo

confidently. 'I'm not likely to use my own name, and I've got a bloody marvellous Irish-American accent that I practised for weeks with a tape recorder. Besides, this other mob is completely different from the Provos in Ulster, and they hate one another's guts like all narrow-minded revolutionaries.'

The chief inspector stared at him in growing amazement and realised that for the first time in his life he was face to face with a true professional man of blood, a hunter-killer programmed like a robot, who thought obsessively of killing his enemies and doing it most efficiently. He didn't care about anything but success in his chosen trade. He'd never stop till he himself was killed. Sperling reluctantly conceded what a total waste it would be to have Faldo uselessly confined in a prison cell, when he could be happily fulfilling his bloody destiny in Ireland for the short time that was left to him.

Let him have his head with the blood-bath.

'Well, it's your own funeral, Faldo,' he said. 'I'm sure you wouldn't expect me to wish you luck. The achievement of people like you I can certainly live without.'

The publishers hope that this book has given you enjoyable reading. Large Print Books are especially designed to be as easy to see and hold as possible. If you wish a complete list of our books please ask at your local library or write directly to:

**Dales Large Print Books**
Magna House, Long Preston,
Skipton, North Yorkshire.
BD23 4ND

This Large Print Book, for people
who cannot read normal print,
is published under the auspices of

## THE ULVERSCROFT FOUNDATION